Don't Tell Anyone I Read Romance

Hatfield Falls (Don't Tell) Book 3

Annilee Nelson

Leenie B Books
Halifax

ISBNs: 978-1-990607-36-3 (ebook); 978-1-990607-37-0 (paperback); 978-1-990607-38-7 (large print)

www.leeniebbooks.com

www.annileenelson.com

Chapter 1

EDMUND BENNET WRAPPED HIS hand firmly around the door handle, then, drawing in a deep breath and holding it to tamp down the touch of anxiety fluttering along his nerves, he slowly and silently pulled open the door that separated the back rooms of the library from the public areas. He had always been good at spying on his older brothers – well, except for his twin since Fred had usually been spying with him.

Surely, he could find out if Ava was here without being noticed, couldn't he?

He peeked his head out, glanced right, then left, and sighed in relief.

She wasn't here. At least, not right here or any place that could be seen from here.

If she was at the library – and he was pretty certain she was since he thought that he had seen her car in the parking lot – she was likely where she always was, in the computer room, which was nowhere near this door. However, one could not be too cautious when attempting to keep from being noticed.

"Are you trying to avoid someone?"

Eddie jumped, and the door thumped against his shoulder. "Ow."

"Sorry," came from somewhere to his left.

"Josh?"

The lanky highschooler who worked part time at the library was leaning against the wall in between two bookcases to the left of the door to the back room. If it hadn't been for his size thirteen red sneakers poking out at the bottom of the bookcase and the fact that he was just head and shoulders taller than the short shelving units, Eddie never would've seen him.

"Why are you standing there?" Eddie rubbed his sore shoulder.

"I was just taking a break," Josh said with a crooked grin as he pushed his glasses up his nose. "And I didn't feel like talking to anyone, so I picked quiet companions." He motioned to the rows of reference books at his side. "They don't get much company, you know."

That was true. The internet was where people went these days to research things. Therefore, these books rarely got used, and Eddie had to admit that the kid had picked a great hiding spot.

"Is your shoulder okay?"

Even though he wanted to keep rubbing his shoulder until the stinging stopped, Edmund let his hand fall to his side. Josh tended to get fixated on things like injuries, and Eddie really wasn't in the mood to be asked every day – at least twice per day – for the rest of the week if his shoulder hurt. "It's just a little bruise if anything at all."

"Sorry about that. I really didn't mean to startle you. I thought you saw me. Do you need some ice? I could go get you an ice pack."

"Nah, I don't need any ice." He just needed to get to the front desk and back without being seen by Ava and talking to Josh about a possible bruised shoulder was not going to help him accomplish that. The longer he stayed in an observable spot, the more likely it was that someone, such as Ava, would see him. He could just duck back inside the back room, but that seemed silly since he needed those books from the front desk if he wanted to clear his list of books to be processed or fixed.

"You're sure?"

"Positive." Eddie took a step away from the safety of the back room where Ava was not allowed to be and towards the books he needed to retrieve.

"So, were you looking for someone?" Josh fell into step along side him.

"I thought you wanted a quiet break."

Josh's watch buzzed at the very moment Eddie finished his comment.

"It's over." Josh held up his arm with the watch on it. "That girl you keep talking to is here again."

"Is she?" So the car he could just see the tail end of from the window in the breakroom was hers. Just as he'd suspected.

"Yep. She's working on the computer next to your grandmother."

That was also what he had expected. Next to his grandmother was Ava's usual spot to work when she was at the library. The two had grown to be good friends from their first meeting, which was not unusual for his grandmother. She made friends easily.

"I heard her ask Lacey if you were here today."

Eddie groaned inwardly as Josh continued his report.

"Lacey said you were in the back and that she'd let you know that she was looking for you."

Eddie blew out a breath. Apparently, no amount of stealth was going to save him from having to see Ava, and he had gotten a bruised shoulder for no reason. He glanced to his right, but his companion was not there.

Josh had stopped walking and was staring at him as if Eddie were the oddest thing he had ever seen. "Is that who you're trying to avoid? The pretty girl?"

Eddie stopped for a moment to reply. "Yeah."

"That's weird. I wouldn't be avoiding her. She's nice."

"She is." And pretty, just as Josh had said. And argumentative. And a romance writer, who had sent him some pages to edit last week and probably wanted to know what he thought of those pages.

"Then, it's even weirder that you're avoiding her."

It wasn't weird at all when you knew that your opinion of her work was likely not going to be well-received, but Eddie wasn't about to tell Josh that. That'd be way too close to telling someone he was reading romance – for pay, but still. It was reading romance, and that was something he'd said he'd never do.

"I just have a lot to do today." Eddie pushed down the twinge of guilt that accompanied the lie. His work was done except for three books that needed protective covers added to them before they went into circulation. "But I suppose I can see what Ava wants first."

There really wasn't any other option. Both his sister-in-law Lacey and Gran would ask him about why he hadn't talked to her. There was a lot that was good about being close to home and family, but then, there were days, like today, when he wished he lived and worked further from home than he did. Maybe he should see if any of the schools were looking for a librarian. Then, none of his family would be able to visit him during his workday – at least not until they had kids in that school, and maybe not even then depending on visitor regulations and such.

"Can I help with any of your work?" Josh offered. He was a good kid in that way. Very obliging and willing to put himself out for someone else. "I did all the shelving that was on the cart, and there's still half-an-hour before I can start going through the bookshelves in there." He thumbed to his right. "To search for books that are out of order."

In the children's area, Eddie could see Jenna weaving her way in between tables where a half-dozen elementary school kids were bent over books doing homework or whatever. To send Josh with his grade ten "geeky cuteness," as Eddie had heard one of the older elementary girls describe it, into the area to look for wayward books would not help Jenna keep things in the afterschool program running as they were supposed to.

"I'm afraid I don't have anything I can pass on to someone else. I'd hate for either you or me to get in trouble." Edmund paused as his eyes roved the library, looking for something for Josh to do that wasn't following him and possibly overhearing that he read romance.

Ah! There! A magazine lay open on a chair. "I don't know if the magazines have been checked yet today. There were quite a few moms here waiting for story time to end earlier. If you could check that, it'd be a big help."

A broad, but still lopsided, grin spread across Josh's face. "I can do that. Thanks, Mr. – er… Eddie," Josh corrected.

Finally. It had taken a full summer and a month and a half of the school year, but Josh had finally remembered that he could call him Eddie and not Mr. Bennett.

As Josh hurried away towards the magazine racks, Eddie turned toward the computer room where Gran was waving him over. She must have been watching for him. He shook his head. There really was no hiding from family some days, and whether his insides were twisting with anxiety or not, the time had come. It couldn't be avoided any longer. He was going to have to tell Ava that her new story was dull – done before – not what would hold a reader's attention – and she wasn't going to like it. Not that he blamed her. He never liked hearing his work was anything but good either.

"Hey, Gran," he said as he entered the computer work room, "how's the computer treating you today?" Yesterday, the cord had come unplugged in the middle of a baking video Gran was watching.

"I've kept my feet very close to my chair and my cane is by the wall, so there was nothing to frighten it into silence." She favoured him with a smile that twinkled in her eyes. She tried his patience at times, but was there really any better grandmother in the whole world that he could have been stuck with? He didn't think so.

"I'm afraid you won't get to climb under the table on my account today," she continued.

Eddie chuckled. "I think I can live with that. Brandon should be here soon."

"Are you trying to get rid of me before my time is up?"

"No, I was just making conversation." And avoiding Ava for as long as possible.

Gran's eyes shifted in Ava's direction as if she could read Eddie's mind. "As much as I love talking to you, there is someone here who wanted your help with something." Her eyebrows waggled.

She knew.

How did she know? This work arrangement between him and Ava was supposed to be confidential. But then, she was Gran. Was there any secret in their family that his grandmother didn't manage to discover? She was excessively good at it. Perhaps she had been a spy in her younger years. His eyes narrowed as he looked at her. Maybe she still was. Who would suspect a loveable, grey-haired lady with a cane of being a secret operative?

"I think she sent you a chapter or two?" There was a lift to her voice that made is sound as if she wasn't sure of the information that Eddie was certain she knew quite well.

Eddie nodded. "She did, but I'm not sure she wants to speak about them with an audience." He gave his grandmother an I-don't-want-to-talk-about-this-now look.

"Well, if you would've replied to the two emails she sent this week, you wouldn't need to speak about it with an audience of one."

His eyes squeezed shut. He had known avoiding those emails was a bad idea, and he had expected Ava to be displeased that he hadn't replied. However, he hadn't expected to be scolded by Gran. He despised being scolded – by anyone – but most especially Gran.

"I'm sorry," he admitted softly. "I just didn't know how to say what I had to say." He still wasn't sure he did.

"You hated them?" Ava's eyes were wide when he finally dared to look in her direction.

"No, not really."

Her arms crossed over her chest – that was Ava's usual prove-me-wrong gesture – and one eyebrow arched over accusing eyes. "*Not really* is the same as *yes*."

"No, it's not."

"Yes, it is."

"Children," Gran inserted. "I think there is an overlap that makes you both correct. Now, sit down, Eddie, and explain yourself, because I liked them."

Eddie's attention snapped to his grandmother and away from the feisty blonde who was still staring him down. "You read them?"

Gran shrugged and nodded as is she wasn't altogether sure she should be admitting to anything.

"She's beta reading for me. I thought it might help me to hear a reader's point of view as I went."

Eddie shifted his focus back to Ava. "And I'm not a reader?"

Ava huffed. Her arms were still crossed, and her expression hadn't softened. "You're an editor and *not* a fan of romance. Gran, on the other hand, *looooves* a good happily ever after."

"I sure do – whether it's in a book or real life." His grandmother winked at him, causing him to shake his head.

His grandmother was nearly as bad as his mother about wanting to see him and his brothers married. Of course, she seemed to be a bit sneakier about it. She wormed her way into the good graces of the young lady she wanted to claim as a granddaughter and then set her course to see it happen. He glanced at Ava and then back to his grandmother. Was this why his Gran had become such good friends with Ava? "Yes, well, let's stick to the fictional ones, shall we?"

No matter how pretty Ava was, he wasn't going to marry a romance author. Not even if she was excessively attractive and her books were good. It just wouldn't work. They argued far too much for them to ever be anything other than acquaintances or perhaps friends. Maybe even good friends.

"You're not getting any younger," Gran grumbled.

"Brandon is older than me, and for that matter, so is Fred."

His grandmother laughed. "Brandon I will concede to, but Fred? I don't think half an hour makes that much of a difference."

"That's not how Fred sees it." Freddie, Eddie's older-by-half-an-hour twin, liked to point out that Eddie was, in fact, the baby brother. At least, there was Emma to take the place of the baby of the family so that he no longer had to be that, too. Not that Emma's arrival had stopped anyone from teasing him about being the baby brother!

"Very well, they are both older than you, but my point still stands. None of you are getting younger and neither am I. I would like to see all of you – even Emma – settled into a happily ever after before I go to my eternal one."

"He doesn't believe happily ever afters exist in reality," Ava said with a flutter of her lashes for him.

"They don't. No one can be happy forever and always." Did they have to argue about this every time it came up? She was wrong. Why couldn't she just accept that happily ever afters, as wonderful as they might be, were fictional.

"That's not what happily ever after means," she retorted as she always did when they ventured down this road.

"That's precisely what happily ever after means – happy forever and always."

"I'm with Ava on this one," Gran inserted, "and I would say half of the Book Drop ladies would agree. The other half would likely view it as narrowly as you do."

"I am not viewing it narrowly." He assumed Ava's prove-me-wrong stance by crossing his arms and scowling. Why was his grandmother taking Ava's side?

"I think you are," Ava muttered.

Of course, she did!

"It's just not possible," he countered.

"I will have you know, Edmund Bennett, that it is entirely possible for a couple to commit themselves to living a happy and satisfied life together." Gran's sharp tone made him wince. "However, that does not mean that everything is smooth sailing. There's often baggage and scars that follow people into marriage. Heaven knows your grandfather and I had our share of disagreements, but we were committed to each other, and we worked it out in such a way that we were quite happy with each other and more than satisfied." Her voice softened. "And when I do step into glory, seeing him again is only second to praising my Saviour on the list of things I want to do."

He wasn't going to win this one. Nor did he really want to win it when his grandmother's voice was so full of emotion. He held up his hands. "Fine. Let's work on the premise that happily ever after means being satisfied and committed."

"And happy," Ava inserted. "Most of the time."

Eddie pressed his lips together and nodded instead of correcting her *most times* to *sometimes*.

"Now, about my pages."

Eddie sat down and ripped the band-aid off the topic. "It's been done before."

Ava shook her head and gave him a wryly amused look. "Of course, it's been done before. There really isn't anything new under the real or the fictional sun."

"That's not what I mean." Oh, he did not want to admit this, but the wound was already exposed. This was going to be painful – and not just for her. "If you give your readers the same plot rewashed and hung out to dry with a little less colour than before, you're going to lose them."

"Did you just say the plot is dull?" Horror painted her features as he nodded.

"I didn't find it dull," Gran inserted.

He blew out a breath. Now came the part of this that would hurt him the most. "Have you read book three?" he asked his grandmother. "This is the same conflict with different names."

Ava's hand clutched his arm. "You read book three?" Her excitement was palpable.

"Yes. I've read this whole series and your last one, too." He squeezed his eyes closed as if not being able to see anything outside of his head would keep his grandmother and Ava from knowing he had spent hours – many, many hours – secretly doing something which he had always said he would never, ever, in a million years, do – reading romance.

"I only have three series under this pen name. I'm impressed."

And there was the smugness he had expected to hear. He despised being wrong and disliked admitting it even more.

"I know. I just started the third series last week." He dared to look at his grandmother, whose mouth was hanging open. "I had to do my research," he said as he lifted and lowered one shoulder.

That's how it had begun, but then, he had actually enjoyed himself. That was a fact that still disturbed him.

"If I'm going to give Ava good advice about her work, I need to know her work. If I hadn't read book three, then I wouldn't know that this book holds a strong similarity to that one."

"Strong enough to put readers off?" Ava asked.

Eddie shrugged. "Maybe not, but do you want to risk it?"

"How many romance books is that?" Gran asked.

"Twenty," Eddie answered. Twenty romance books were all he was going to admit to having read. There was no way he was going to tell either Ava or Gran that he had subscribed to Ava's mailing list under an alias and a new email address to get the free prequels she offered. He had fully intended to unsubscribe as soon as he got the freebies, and he still might, but he hadn't yet. She was entertaining even in her emails.

"I was surprised when I heard you had read one and were going to help edit when needed. But twenty?" Gran shook her head in unbelief. "Well, if that doesn't prove miracles still happen."

"I wouldn't call it miraculous that I read twenty books."

"I would, and I am since they're romance books," his grandmother replied with a laugh. She patted his knee. "Your secret is safe with me. I'm not going to stand in the way of you helping Ava get those books written. That first one I read was good. I'm glad Trish told us about it at book club."

"I'm glad she talked about it while I was getting a muffin so I could be exempt from the conversation." Ava said before looking at Eddie. "I suppose if I don't want to listen to comments about the new book being dull at a future Book Drop meeting, I need to fix what I've written. Did you have any ideas about how to improve or change it when you were reading it?"

"I did."

"Could you email them to me?"

"Sure."

"This week?" She gave him a pointed look.

He smiled sheepishly. "Yeah. I'll get them to you tomorrow morning. I just really didn't know how to tell you that your chapters weren't as engaging as they should be."

"You seemed plenty capable of doing that just now," she grumbled.

"Because I had to. Not because I wanted to."

He knew she was struggling. How couldn't she be? Her brother-in-law had been killed in a military exercise not that long ago. She was throwing herself into helping her sister deal with her grief and her daughter all while trying to craft happily ever afters for her readers to enjoy.

Happily ever after he scoffed silently. Losing a husband to an accident didn't sound like a happily ever after to him. They just didn't exist in real life, which was one reason why he had never liked romances.

She gave him one of those sweet smiles she often wore when she wasn't being challenging. "Thanks. I'm glad you considered my feelings in the matter, but I do need to know these things. Even if I don't want to." The smile faded.

"Sorry." Necessary or not, it hurt to add to the burden she was carrying.

"No, no, don't be. We're professionals. We can deal with difficult things. Of course, my former editor sometimes sweetened the news with chocolate."

Eddie laughed. "What is it with girls and chocolate?"

"I don't know about other girls, but it's this girl's favourite sweet treat."

"Duly noted. I will try to remember the chocolate the next time I have a tough critique to deliver."

Gran patted his knee again. "Such a good boy," she muttered. "Now, before Brandon gets here, do you know if book three is available in paperback?"

"No, but I can look." His grandmother preferred paperbacks to ebooks just like he did. "Are you sure you don't want to start with book one?"

"Wellll…" the word was drawn out and Gran's tone was uncertain. "I really want to know if what you said about book three and the newest chapters is as obvious to me as it is to you, but I suppose starting with book one makes sense." She nodded her head as if she had made some sort of decision. "Yes, I do believe you are correct, so, if books one through three are available, I think I have my next three weeks' reading sorted, and I can go back to the other series that other book was part of after."

"Do you need anything else?" Eddie asked Ava as he stood.

"No, just that email tomorrow."

"You'll have it," he assured her before going to see what he could find for Gran.

Chapter 2

AVA HUNG HER JACKET in the closet and slipped her feet out of her boots and into her slippers. Then, she scratched behind the ears of the ball of fur that was shivering and occasionally barking with excitement at her feet. It didn't matter if she was gone for five minutes or several hours, Charlie, whose true name was Charlotte, was always irrepressibly happy to see her come home.

"How was your day at the library? Any new books ready to read?" Her sister, Ali, called to her from the playroom.

"No, I'm still working on an Avery-Anne one, but hopefully by spring it will be sitting proudly on your shelf." Ava crossed the kitchen to the room where her sister was sitting on the floor with Riley. "How's my Peanut today?' she asked her niece as she climbed over the baby gate.

Riley took the plastic cookie from her mouth and offered it to Ava.

"Yeah, as nice as it is for you to share, I think a cookie so close to dinner time might not be good for me." Slick-with-slobber, fake cookies were not on Ava's list of things she ever wanted to eat or even really touch. Babies sure did produce a lot of drool when they were teething, but, according to Ali, that part of Riley's life was growing to a close.

Riley babbled something unintelligible and then, looked at Ava as if she expected a response. Ava shook her head. "I'm sorry, Peanut, but I didn't understand that."

"She wants chicken for supper and was telling you about it."

"How do you do that?" Ava looked with wonder at her sister. It seemed Ali always knew what Riley was chattering about.

"Tick-tick is chicken," Ali replied with a shrug. "If you spend enough time with her, you catch on to what she's trying to say." Her smile faltered, and she looked away. It was a pretty good sign that she had some news she did not want to divulge. Ava might not understand eighteen-month-old toddler gibberish, but she knew her sister's unspoken language.

"What did you do while Aunt Ava was gone?" she asked Riley, ignoring what she really wanted to know in favour of waiting until Ali was ready to broach the subject of whatever it was. "Did you take a nap?"

Riley's nose wrinkled up and started to babble again.

"You still don't like naps, huh?" Ava might not know what her niece was saying, but from the tone of voice she was using, she was not pleased.

"No, she doesn't. However, her mom would love one now and then." Ali stifled a yawn.

"Do you want to lie down now? I can make dinner without you."

"No, I'm good. I'd like an edible dinner."

Ava laughed. Her sister wasn't being harsh. It was true that Ava was no culinary master – far from it!

Ali pushed up from the floor. "That being said, I wouldn't mind a trip to the bathroom without an audience."

Ava giggled. "I've gotcha covered." She picked up a cup and saucer from Riley's play set. "Could I please have some tea?"

"May I," her sister threw over her shoulder. "You would think that you, of all people, would get that right."

"That's why I have an editor," Ava called back before returning her attention to Riley. "May I have some tea, please?" She held out her cup so that Riley could pretend to pour some tea into it. "Thank you, miss. Have you had any callers today?"

Riley's head bobbed up and down as she toddled over to the play stove. She babbled about something as she started stacking pots and blocks and various other toys on it.

"Car bye-bye."

Ava tipped her head. Intelligible words, but what did that mean? "Did you go for a drive in the car today?" That seemed like a possible meaning, right?

"Car bye-bye." Riley held out her empty hands towards Ava as if to say she didn't know why Aunt Ava didn't understand her.

"Is that a *yes* or a *no*?"

"It's a yes," Ali answered. "I dropped off a resume today, and Riley went with me."

"A resume? Are you looking for a job?" She hadn't expected her sister to do that for a while longer. It really hadn't been all that long since she had become a single mother.

Ali shrugged and nodded. "I need to get out of this house more, and the life insurance and all that won't last forever. And Riley could use to be with other kids more than just on Sunday."

"I can take her to story time at the library both here and in Hatfield Falls," Ava offered.

"I know, but…" She pressed her lips together. "We should start making dinner."

That was Ali's code for she had more to say but not with her daughter present.

"Do you want music or a video?" Ava asked Riley and then, looked to her sister for interpretation of the response.

"T-t is Thomas."

"Ok, then. *Thomas the Tank Engine* it is." Ava pulled up the app on her phone that was connected to the TV streaming service and found the list of *Thomas and Friends* episodes. Thomas was a favourite with Riley, or so it seemed since that was what was most often playing while Ava and her sister made dinner.

"Which one?" She held the phone so Riley could see it. "Just touch one. Gently."

Riley poked a pudgy little finger on a picture, and the episode popped onto the television screen.

As Ava left the room, Riley was doing a little dance in a circle and clapping her hands as the opening song filled the air.

"She's so sweet," she said as she stood at the door between the playroom and kitchen. She often found herself watching Riley with a wistful, happy feeling. Well, when Riley wasn't being disagreeable, that is. Maybe one day she'd have her own sweet little bundle of drool and babble – if she could ever find a guy who was willing to marry her.

"She is, but make sure that gate is secure so her sweetness stays in the other room."

"You're not ready to teach her how to cook tick-tick?"

Ali laughed. "I barely have you making it right. I think we need to work on that before I start trying to teach a child whose attention span is shorter than yours and whose ability to listen to directions is only marginally better."

"What?" Ava asked with a teasing grin.

"Precisely. Now, grab the tick-tick, buttermilk, and eggs while I get this breading mix ready."

"Oooh," Ava said as she pulled boneless, skinless chicken breasts from the fridge, "tick-tick nuggets?"

Ali laughed. "Yep, I want to keep both my girls happy tonight."

"You want to keep us happy every night," Ava replied, "but I have to admit I'm a touch happier when dinner is tick-tick nuggets."

Ali laughed. "I know, and since I have to tell you something you might not like, I was hoping this would help."

Ava stacked the carton of buttermilk on top of the eggs and chicken she held and pushed the refrigerator door closed with her foot. "Go on. What am I not going to like?"

"I had a realtor come over today."

"You're selling the house?"

Ali shrugged and stirred the cornmeal, flour, and spice dredge vigorously. "I think so."

A whoosh of air escaped Ava. "What did the realtor say?"

"She noted a few things that I should maybe get fixed before I put the house on the market if I want to get the best price, and she said that spring would be the best time to sell, but if we could get things updated now, we might be able to find an interested buyer sooner, and then she warned me that things tend to slow down around the holidays and in January."

"Okay." Wow. Ava never expected her sister to move out of this house unless Frank had gotten posted somewhere else. Even then, the two of them had spoken about keeping it as a rental until Frank was ready to retire from the military. But Frank was gone now, so... Ava wouldn't let her thoughts wander down that path very far. "When do you think you'll list it?"

Ali sighed. "I might wait until spring. It might be nice to have one more Christmas here, although..." She turned and leaned against the counter. "There are so many memories here." Her lips trembled. "Some days I want to just be wrapped in those memories and never leave them, and other days, I want to burn them down so they can't hurt me anymore. Maybe I need a fresh start? Ya know?"

Ava nodded. What else was she supposed to do? Tell her sister that a fresh start would not take away all the pain? Whether it was true or not, that didn't seem like a good idea.

"I think," Ali continued, "that it might be good for me to find a new, smaller place near a school I want to send Riley to – maybe even one that has a daycare close by so I can send her a couple of days a week while I start to get my feet under me as a working mom."

"I thought you wanted her to go to the same schools we went to?"

Again, Ali heaved a deep sigh. This time when her lips trembled, she had to wipe a tear from her cheek. "I don't know if I could handle walking through those halls where Frank and I became friends as kids."

Ali placed a piece of chicken on the cutting board and began slicing it into nugget-size pieces.

"Some of the same teachers we had are still at the elementary school. I don't want to hear about Frank every time I drop Riley off or pick her up."

"That would be hard, but then, what's easy about this, right?"

"You can say that again." Ali put the pan she needed on the counter. "I'm not running away from things. I promise you that I'm not. I just need some space. A little distance between me and what was and was going to be."

"I guess I can understand that."

"Do you know how many times I hear a truck go by and think it must be Frank coming home?"

Ava shook her head. "But won't that be the same no matter where you are?"

Ali shrugged. "Maybe, but Frank was here. He won't be wherever we go next." She stood looking at Ava while putting on a pair of gloves to start the messy work of coating the chicken. "Maybe I'll find out I'm wrong, but I've been praying about it, and I keep getting drawn to the idea of moving. I don't want to be stuck where I'm not supposed to be – and before you say it, no, I'm not just being drawn to what I want. I love this house and this neighbourhood. It's so close to Mom and Dad and then, there's you. I love sharing my life with you. I told the realtor that I wouldn't make a decision one way or the other until I've had time to carefully consider things and talk to all those who this decision will affect."

She pulled her lip between her teeth and gave Ava a pleading look.

"Oh, no! I'm not breaking this news to Mom and Dad. You're going to have to do that. However, I will help you make the dinner and even hold your hand while you tell them if you need me to."

Her sister's nose scrunched up just like Riley's had when Ava had asked her about taking a nap. The expression was accompanied by a huff.

"You know you have to do it, right?" Ava pressed. "I'd likely get all the reasons wrong or present it in a way that doesn't represent what you're thinking. I'm good at fiction, Ali, not real life."

"You seem pretty good at real life to me. You run your own business and make a living doing it."

"It's only a living if I can afford my living expenses."

Ali rolled her eyes and made a sound of disbelief.

"Well, it's true!"

"You'll remember that I know how much you make. It's not caviar on toast with champagne –"

"Ew!"

Ali laughed. "I know, I know, but you get what I'm saying, right?"

"Yeah," Ava agreed reluctantly. "It's more squeeze cheese on crackers with a soda."

"You do love squeeze cheese. Remember how excited you used to get at Christmas when Mom would buy a can of that cheese and the 'fancy' crackers?"

It was Ava's turn to laugh. "Remember it? I still get excited when I see she has that on the table while we open presents."

"Are you okay with me moving forward? I know it will also mean a shift in housing for you."

Ava looked at the quartz countertop and the two-tone cabinets. Then, she turned to look out at the well-treed yard before letting her eyes rest on the table in the eating nook on the other side of the kitchen.

This house was so comfortable – and not just because her sister lived here. It was just so well laid out and decorated.

Maybe Eddie was right. Maybe happily ever afters were fantasy. After all, this was supposed to be the setting for Ali's happily ever after.

"I won't say that I won't miss it and what we've had here, but yeah, I'd never want to hold you back from what you need to be as happy as you possibly can be." Tears pricked her eyes. "I guess you'll miss the same thing, huh?"

Ali nodded.

"Frank would want you to be happy. He never liked being the reason you cried, so if moving is needed, then, move – whenever and wherever you want." Ava hugged her sister from behind as Ali wiped at her tears with her sleeve.

"Just let them fall in the batter," Ava whispered in her ear. "A little extra salt might be tasty."

Ali gave her a shove with her elbow. "You're a dork."

"I know, but you love me anyway."

"I most certainly do. Now, tell me something you did today that will help me stop crying. Was Mrs. Green at the library again today?"

"She was, and she liked my chapters. Unfortunately, my editor was not as pleased with them."

"The new editor?" Ali's tone dripped with shock.

"Yep. He said what I wrote was too much like what I've already written."

Ali held the gloves she had removed over the trash bin and turned slowly toward Ava. "He? Your new editor is a *he*?"

"Yeah, he's a *he*." A very attractive, if somewhat annoying and often wrong about romance, *he*, and yet, she'd still go out with him if he asked her. There was just something about him that spoke of possibilities and happy forevers.

"Huh? Do you think maybe he'd like your pages better if he was not a *he*?"

Ava might have thought the same thing if she didn't know Eddie had read nearly all of her Avery-Anne books. "Nope. I actually think he might be right, but I'll save my final opinion until after he sends me his notes tomorrow."

The same went for his opinion about happily ever afters. She wasn't ready to give up on them any more than she was willing to toss aside her love of writing because the cute guy she had a crush on said her book needed work. Perhaps there was a way to fix both her book and his erroneous opinion.

Chapter 3

"Whatcha doing?" Fred popped his head into Eddie's room in the basement of the split-entry house they shared with their next oldest brother Henry.

Eddie turned his laptop so that Fred wouldn't see what he was reading. "Just working on an editing project." Sort of. If one counted reading all the books an author had ever written as part of being her editor.

"Yeah?" Fred crossed the room and sat on the edge of the bed that was closest to Eddie's desk. "Anything good?"

"Actually, yes." The more he read Ava's books, the more he feared he might be in danger of falling in love with reading romance novels.

"Any insider info about the next breakout bestseller?"

"I can't divulge secrets; you know that." Eddie closed the laptop as his phone dinged.

"Why is Trish's friend Ava texting you about chocolate?"

Eddie snatched the phone from next to Fred, looked at the chocolate bar and happy emoji Ava had sent, and then, shoved the phone in his pocket. "She hangs out with Gran."

Fred nodded slowly. "I know that, but that doesn't answer anything." His eyes narrowed. "Wait. Are you secretly dating her like Will did with Lacey?"

Eddie laughed. "No. She's not my type."

Fred lay back on the bed, and Eddie took the spot next to him. "She's cute."

"And opinionated." And confident. She simply oozed the stuff. Unlike him. Sure, people thought he was confident, but he doubted many of them knew how much effort it had taken to become who he now was.

"Yeah? Guess I haven't talked to her enough to know that."

Eddie's phone dinged again. He checked it. Ava. "She had a project for me to look over for her, so I gave her my number." That was completely true.

"She writes?"

Eddie nodded as he read Ava's message about how much she had enjoyed the chocolate. Then, he sent a smiley face and the message: *Tell Gran thanks for giving it to you and not eating it before you got there.*

"You gave her chocolate?"

Eddie pulled his phone away from where Fred could see it. "Nosey much?"

"Hey, it was right there."

"Didn't mean you had to read it."

"Sorry, but we've always shared everything until recently." Fred sighed. "I don't like it. I mean, it had to happen eventually, I suppose, but I don't like it."

"If it helps, I don't like it either." But he just couldn't let Fred know what sort of "project" he was editing for Ava. He couldn't.

Fred was the cool half of the pair that they made. Eddie was the nerd who loved books and diagramming sentences, but he had worked hard to carve out a dignified nerd persona. He had managed to mould the things he liked into an image of a sophisticated fellow with elevated tastes. Or so he'd like to think he had. And letting more than Ava and Gran know that he had read genre fiction – the sort that required a happy ending – and that he had done it of his own accord and not because he had been assigned to do so, well, that wouldn't help him keep up that image, now would it?

Fred shrugged. "I guess that makes it marginally better."

"The chocolate was because she told me her former editor often softened the blow of criticism with it, and my feedback to her wasn't exactly glowing."

"Right. You said she is a writer of some sort?" There was an upward lift to Fred's statement, making it more of a question.

"Yep, she is." And that was all he was going to admit to. "Did you work today?"

"Nope. I spent the day looking at apartments. I know Trish said she doesn't want us to move out on account of her and Henry getting married, but..."

"Hey, you don't have to convince me that it would be awkward to stay here." It was bad enough walking into the kitchen on a movie night when a large crowd was gathered in the living room and finding his brother and Trish wrapped up in each other. He'd rather not have to be privy to any more amorous interludes – especially since the "not-yet-married" boundaries that Henry and Trish had in place now would be gone then.

"I saw a couple two-bedroom apartments that might work if you're still interested in sharing a place." He gave Eddie a teasing smile. "Guess I should add that I could handle the whole rental amount if you decide to copy Henry and find a bookish girl to marry."

Eddie shook his head. "I'm just doing some editing for Ava."

"Yep, and Will and Lacey were just friends. At least, Henry never hid that he liked Trish."

"Seriously, it's just editing."

"If you say so." He gave Eddie a look that said there was nothing that could be said to convince him that Eddie wasn't secretly in love with Ava.

In love was a bit too far – found her attractive and thought about her far too often, now those were closer to the truth of the matter. But that was nothing. He'd found many females attractive and captivating over the years. Ava was a character study – a pretty one – nothing else.

"Now, about the places I looked at. They're nice, but I've been thinking that maybe I'd like to do what Henry did and find a place to fix up a bit and own rather than giving all my money to a landlord. I mean, it hasn't been bad paying Henry, but I don't know that I want to continue to pay someone forever."

"Not even if that someone is Will?" Eddie had always thought he'd like to have his eldest brother as a landlord if he wasn't in the position to purchase property of his own. Will did everything by the book when it came to leasing places. His tenants had to be some of the happiest ever. At least, he had never heard any complaints from those who he knew rented from Will.

Fred shook his head. "The places I viewed weren't Bennett Homes properties. Will said he didn't have any rentals open or coming open soon."

See, he was right. Will's tenants were happy.

"However..." Fred leaned forward. "He does know of a place that might be a good possible flip, and he said that he and Nate would be willing to pass on the place if I'm interested enough. Of course, I'd get them to help me with what renos I could squeeze out of my budget, so they wouldn't be losing out completely."

"You can afford that? I thought you didn't think you'd be able to buy anything for at least another year?" Both he and Fred had been saving money for future housing while paying Henry to live in his basement, and they had both planned to be able to move out and have their own places in a year or two.

Fred nodded. "I think I can unless there's a bidding war or something."

"Have you seen the place yet?"

"Nah, and that's why I need you."

"Me? Why?"

"Well, you'll be living with me for a while I hope, and I value your opinion." He added a cheesy grin at the end of his comments that said there was more to it.

"And..." Eddie folded his arms and cocked an eyebrow over a look of disbelief. "What's the real reason?"

"You know that Will is working with a new realtor, right?"

Ah. That made sense. "Tiffany Martin? She's the reason you need me to go with you?"

"Yeah. You're not working tonight, and Will and Nate are both busy. So..."

"Tonight?"

"More like in half an hour."

"Half an hour? I have a manuscript to read." Not that he had a deadline for getting it read and not that the manuscript was not already a book, but still. He didn't particularly want to go anywhere tonight. It was cold, and his track pants were comfy.

"Please?"

"Do you seriously think she would flirt with you while showing you a house? She strikes me as more professional than that." From what he had seen, it appeared as if image was as important to Tiffany as it was to him. "Besides, I don't think she's the sort to marry a mechanic." She looked like she'd only settle for someone with a designer suit or two in their closet. That wasn't Fred.

"Come on," Fred begged. "You'll be living there, too. You know you're going to want to see it."

That was a reason that made sense. "Fine. I'll put this away and put on some jeans."

"Henry is taking Trish out tonight, so you want to grab something to eat on the way home so that I don't have to cook when we get back?"

"Are you sure *that's* not the reason you want me to go with you – so you can ditch cooking?"

Fred laughed. "No, though it's a perk. We can't all be you and Emma." He stood at the door to Eddie's bedroom. "Thanks for being willing to do this with me." He shrugged and looked rather uneasy, which for Freddie wasn't normal. "Facing a new and potentially big purchase decision seems easier when you're with me. Meet you at my car."

Well, that explained the unease. Admitting a fear wasn't easy. That's why Eddie rarely shared his fears with anyone other than their dad. Occasionally, he'd tell Fred, but Dad seemed safer. Dad wouldn't tease him about it. Dads were just different than brothers.

~*~

Three-quarters of an hour later, Fred pulled his car into a driveway in a community of older style houses. This one was a bungalow that would have looked right at home as part of the set of one of those old television shows their mom like to watch.

"Mom would like it."

Eddie laughed. "That's exactly what I was thinking."

"Which means it definitely needs updating, especially if the inside looks as vintage as the outside looks."

"The lawn is tidy. So, I'd guess the owner cared for the place." Eddie pushed his door open and started to get out of the car.

"Oh, I see you were able to get your brother to join you." Tiffany had come to meet them at the car. "It will make it easier to make a quick decision on this if you both get to see the place. Sandra doesn't want to keep this a pocket listing for long. She'd really like to set up a weekend of tours and bidding, but she also knows that keeping your older brother happy is good for business."

Eddie's brow furrowed. How was showing a house to him and Fred going to keep Will happy?

"She doesn't want to give him any reason to go with a different realtor for his new project, and he and Nate have purchased several reno projects from her in the past," she explained as she motioned for them to proceed toward the door in front of her. "The door is open so go right in."

"Whoa," Fred muttered as he stepped into the house ahead of Eddie. "Time warp or what?"

While there was a small patch of linoleum at the entrance, the door led them into a cozy living room that boasted flowered wallpaper and a shaggy pink carpet.

"The house is priced as it is because the owner knows that whoever buys it will need to do some work. She hasn't touched it in years."

"As if you needed to tell me that," Fred said with a laugh. "What do you think, Eddie, should we keep the pink carpet?"

Eddie shook his head. "No, I don't see anything to keep."

Tiffany smiled. "Neither do I. In fact, let me give you some suggestions as we go through. There isn't room to extend out the back too far due to regulations regarding footprint, but you *could* add a little bit square footage that direction, or a whole lot more by going up. Not that you need to do either of those things unless you wanted to expand for a family at some point in the future. That fireplace is currently only for decoration and as you can see, the kitchen is a gut job. I really don't think those cabinets are worth trying to salvage, but you might think otherwise based on budget. And, of course, you'll want new appliances."

She stood in the middle of a postage stamp size kitchen with orange-y brown cupboards that had ceramic knobs and pulls on them. Did Fred actually think he could afford to buy this place and fix it up? Eddie frowned. He hated to be the bad guy here, but he wasn't seeing anything to make him want to promote the place to his brother.

"I can see you might need a little convincing," Tiffany said to him. "There are three bedrooms and one bath on this level and a possible fourth bedroom and half bath in the basement. I'm not going to say this place is going to need just a coat of paint and new floors to get it up to livable by what I've seen of Will and Nate's standards." She gave him and Fred a questioning look.

"Yeah, that'd describe what we like pretty well, though I might be a little less picky than Will." He tipped his head towards Eddie. "He's not. He's got an eye for classier stuff than I do."

Tiffany's smile grew at that comment. "Well, then, let me describe this to Eddie and see if it's something he'd like."

For thirty minutes, she walked them through the house and backyard describing what was possible, from a new floor layout in the living spaces, to losing a bedroom to make a primary suite, to creating a second primary suite in the basement with an added entrance that led out to a patio.

"And this," she said standing just at the back of the house, "this is where I'd put a garage. It would mean extending the driveway, but it would be worth it in the winter or for when you need to do a bit of work on the brakes or something."

Oh, she was good. While a new kitchen with an island was not something that would inspire Fred to purchase a home, a garage with space to work on his car was.

Eddie watched his brother turn and look at the house and then back to the future garage. "That's a lot of stuff to be done. I don't know." He rubbed the back of his neck.

"I can have Will and Nate look at it tomorrow and give me a ballpark number for the changes, although I'm pretty sure my guess is right. Then, we can look at the best way to present an offer to get this at asking price and right away." She took out her phone. "This is what you said you had for a down payment, right?" She turned the phone towards Fred, and he nodded. Her purple painted nails clicked on the screen as she typed some numbers into the calculator.

"If we can secure financing, which I assume you will be able to do unless you have too large a debt-to-income ratio or some horrible credit fiasco in your past?"

"Nope, none of that."

"You do have a credit score though, right?"

"I do. Dad made sure we all understood the importance of that."

"Good," she said with a smile. "Then, I would say with the purchase price and everything we talked about at the price I'm thinking it will be, your monthly payment should be this." Again, she turned the phone toward Fred. "That's just inside what you said you could pay for rent. Houses like this and at this price don't come up on the market that often. Sandra was disappointed that she couldn't talk the owner into listing this one for more than it is."

"How long would all the work take?" Eddie asked. "Henry and Trish are getting married in February."

"I'm not going to lie. It'll be a tight timeline considering it's so close to winter, but it might be possible to have at least enough of the renovations done so that you can move in before then. So, do I call Will and Nate and find out if this is a real possibility?"

Fred looked at Eddie. "What do you think?"

"It's your money."

"Yeah, but I don't want to be stupid about it, and you follow your head more than I do."

That was true. Fred was more easily swayed to act impulsively on a feeling.

"It feels good," he added.

"If it fits the budget and the timeline and you like the neighbourhood and the house, then, go for it. I'll live here with you until you kick me out." He gave his brother a warning glare when Fred's lips curled into a teasing grin. Now was not the time to tease him about Ava.

"Okay, then, I say you should call Will and Nate, Tiffany, and we'll go from there."

Chapter 4

"MY SISTER'S MOVING." AVA placed the plate of cookies Gran had given her on the table at the side of the community room where they held their Book Drop meeting.

"She is?" Trish Thompson asked in surprise. "I thought you said she loved her house and would never leave it."

"That's what I thought, but..." Ava lifted and lowered her shoulders in a shrug as she blew out a breath. "I mean, I get it, I suppose. There are too many memories locked up in the place, but..." Again, her voice trailed off, this time on a soft sigh.

Ali's house had always been the fairytale princess's home in Ava's mind. The place where all would be made right in the world because love dwelled within its walls. It was what she had always dreamed of having – a home of her own where love wrapped her in its warm embrace and buoyed her above any dark thoughts. But as she had been learning since she turned thirteen, just because she could imagine something, it didn't follow that she could create it on anything other than paper.

"When does she want to move?" Lacey Bennett asked as she fanned out the napkins next to the cookie trays.

The three of them – Ava, Lacey, and Trish – always met early each month before the book club meeting and made sure the community room at Gran's apartment complex was ready – sweets on trays, napkins at the ready, and a jug of water and some cups for those who chose not to BYOB (bring your own beverage).

Lacey and Trish were new friends, but Ava honestly couldn't remember ever having met friends that felt like family so quickly as these two did. She felt as comfortable around them as she did Nikki, who had been her BFF since grade three. Had it only been a little more than half a year ago that she had met Trish and Lacey at the Hatfield Falls Library?

Gran, the most likely reason for them all feeling like sisters rather than just friends, opened the door to the community room. "I've got the last plate of sweets – lemon squares from Dorothy." She gave them each a questioning look. "This glum mood is not a good way to start. What's up?"

"My sister is going to sell her house – maybe before Christmas, maybe after. She's not sure yet."

"Wow, that's soon," Lacey said.

Ava nodded.

"I almost sold my house when my husband died," Gran said. "But Amy was getting older, and I knew she wouldn't be around home for long. I didn't want to make things harder for her, so I stayed put and did some renovations to make the place feel different." Her lips tipped into a crooked smile. "It didn't erase the memories, but it put up a bit of a barrier to soften them in my mind, which in turn made them less painful. I'm glad I kept it as long as I did, but it wasn't easy at first."

Gran slipped her arm around Ava's and led her to the circle of chairs and sofas in the middle of the room. "The memories will go with her, but they might be more bearable in a different home. It might even help her find a way to make room for a possible new family."

"I know. I know it's a good thing, but I'm not going to say it will be an easy transition for me. I'll need to find a new place to live, and for nearly the first time in my life, it'll be a place without her."

Ali had only lived in a house different from where Ava lived for one year before Riley was born. Even then, she would have Ava over for sleepovers when Frank was away on deployment. Those sleepovers had become a permanent arrangement once Riley was born, and Frank had insisted it was a good idea for Ali to have someone close by to help. That's when they had remodeled part of the basement into a studio apartment for her.

"Cari has a spare room, and Trish won't need her place in February," Lacey offered. "And Will always has something he knows about that might work. We'll make sure you're not homeless."

Lacey's husband, Will, and his friend Nate were into property investments, and he was good at his job. But success was not measured in dollars and cents in Will's mind – he had said so several times over the course of Ava's acquaintance with him. What drove him was his desire to put loving one's neighbour as oneself into practice, one house or apartment at a time. Cost and fees were kept reasonable, and services were provided to the highest standard he could manage.

"Does he have any houses or apartments near a good preschool and elementary school?"

"For Riley?" Trish asked.

"Yeah, Ali's going to go back to work."

"What kind of work?" Gran asked.

"She's got an office admin certificate."

Gran tipped her head and looked at Lacey.

"I'll mention it to Will and Nate. They might be ready to take someone on," Lacey said. "That is, if Ali wouldn't mind working with a couple of demanding men." She laughed. "Actually, Nate's not that demanding."

Ava and the others joined her in laughing at that. They all knew that Will was the more particular of the two men she was talking about.

"I'll let you know what Will says and then, maybe, you can have your sister send a resume to him."

"Or she can send it to me, and I can pass it on," Gran offered with a chuckle.

"I think I'll let her send it to Will," Ava said. She had heard the story of how Gran had sent Lacey's resume to Will without Lacey's approval back when Lacey wasn't even sure she liked Will enough to work with him.

"Hey, are we the first ones here?" Emma Bennett asked as she and Lacey's sister, Cari, entered the room. "I brought some almond cakes from the café. Cari made them."

The door opened behind them, and Dorothy, the maker of the lemon squares and her friend Clara entered.

Private conversation time was over. For the next hour and a half, they'd be chatting up books and sharing bits of their lives with each other, but the really personal stuff – the stuff that Ava only shared with her sister or closest friends – wouldn't be touched, at least not by her.

A few Book Drop members, such as Dorothy and Gran and even sweet Esther Adams, seemed willing to lay their lives open in front of the group. Ava was not like that. She

had secrets in the form of two pen names which she wished
to keep just that – secret. Maybe the others did, too. It
wasn't like she could see inside their minds. Perhaps they,
like her, were also only sharing the comfortable bits.

"Oh, have I got a book to recommend to you this
month!" Clara said as she placed that book on her chair
and a thermal mug on the floor next to the chair leg before
heading to the sweets table.

Ava shared a look with Trish who was struggling to
conceal a giggle.

"Have you ever read any of those fan fiction books?"
Clara continued as she stacked three cookies and a lemon
square on top of her napkin. Clara was a lady of at least
seventy years and the very picture of a perfect storybook
grandmother: grey hair in a short sassy style, an outfit that
was neither too old nor too young, and a figure that was
softly curved. She also gave the best hugs. Everyone who
was one of the *youngsters* in the group, as she called them,
was given hugs unless they seemed uncomfortable with
such displays of affection. Then, they would receive just a
friendly pat on the shoulder or a squeeze of their hand.

"Fan fiction?" Gran asked. "I'm not sure I know what
that is."

"Oh, I didn't either until recently, but my granddaughter, Josie, is into it. So, I thought I'd take a look at one of
the books she'd read." She picked up the book on her chair
and sat down. "This is that book. Apparently, there are
people who play with the characters and stories of other
authors and publish those new stories. Most, Josie says, are
online, but some like this one actually get made into books
because the stories are old enough or something."

"They're in the public domain," Ava inserted. "That means the copyright on the original work has expired."

Clara smiled at her. "That's what it was that Josie said. I knew there was some legal-type word she had used." She rested her pile of sweets on the table next to her and picked up the book. "This one is what is called an Austen variation."

"Austen?" Gran's eyebrows shot up. "As in Jane Austen?"

Clara nodded. "The very one! And let me tell you, I wish Miss Austen had written as cute a story as this one." She pursed her lips as if she were the queen of the book club waiting to share the most delicious news. "This one is based on..." She leaned forward and looked around the group. "*Mansfield Park*." She sat back, looking quite satisfied with the secret she had shared. "Josie says the next in the series is based on..." Her brow furrowed. "*Emma*, I think?"

"Actually, it's *Northanger Abbey*," Ava corrected.

"Oh, have you read them?"

Ava peeked at Trish. "I have."

"So have I," Trish said. "Although I only borrowed the ebooks from the library. I don't have any paperbacks to share."

"The library has these?" Clara cried in delight. "I thought it was only something Josie could get at one of the malls she likes to visit when she goes to the city." She shook her head. "I don't know why I didn't even think to look at the library first."

"We have the whole series at the library in our ebook collection," Trish continued. "Or at least, we have as much as there is of it at present."

"I should maybe tell Amy about these." Gran had taken the book from Clara and was paging through it. "She loves all things Austen. Although, if she's anything like my grandson Eddie, she might not like anything that alters the original."

"She might like these books then," Trish said. "They don't alter what has happened in the novels. These are set after the novel closes and shows how some of the side characters' lives developed from there."

"Oh, five books? That should keep me reading for a while." Clara had her phone out and was scrolling on the screen. "Book two and three," she said as she tapped, "are now on my to-be-read pile."

"I hear," Trish continued, "that the author has at least two more planned. In fact, she has teased that book six might be out in the spring if all goes well, but she's had some personal things come up that have interfered with her writing schedule."

"Oh! How do you know that?" Clara asked.

Trish shrugged. "Librarian powers."

Clara gave her an exasperated look.

"Ok, so I don't have any special librarian powers," Trish said with a laugh. "I subscribed to her newsletter."

"You can do that?" Dorothy asked. "Does it come in the mail or on the computer?"

Dorothy had just celebrated her eightieth birthday last month and while she used technology, parts of it still baffled her.

"Author newsletters come via email," Esther said as she sat down next to Dorothy. "I can show you how to sign up and all that after our meeting if you want."

Esther was twenty-three, just like Ava, and she was the embodiment of sweetness. She always had a ready smile and a kind, soft word. Ava imagined that her elementary students must fall over themselves to please their teacher.

Ava's brow furrowed. Maybe Ali could find a place near where Esther taught. She'd be more than happy to have Esther teach Riley, and she suspected Ali would be, too. She'd have to mention that to her sister tomorrow, right after she got done telling her about how once again one of her books was a recommendation in their book club.

A few other ladies of various ages had entered the room, but that didn't stop Clara from launching into her review of the book she had brought.

Ava stood. "Save my place," she whispered to Trish.

"You're not sticking around for this review?" she asked in a teasing tone.

"I need cookies." And she might need to either stop writing books or stop attending the Book Drop if she didn't want to spend several minutes of each meeting at the snack table trying to avoid being seen while someone critiqued her book. At this rate, she was going to have to trade in her jeans for the next size up.

When she glanced back at the group of ladies, Gran was watching her.

Gran arched a brow and tipped her head toward Clara.

Ava sighed. How was it that that woman could decipher secrets so easily? Ava lifted and lowered a shoulder before nodding, which caused Gran to grin.

Ava bit into a soft chocolate chip cookie. Her eyes closed as she savoured the flavours of brown sugar and chocolate melting in her mouth. She'd keep writing and attending this group as long as these cookies had her back and offered a sweet escape when the conversation became uncomfortable. Even if it meant shopping for new jeans.

Chapter 5

"GOOD MORNING, MR. BENNETT."

Edmund turned from filing papers in the cabinet behind the information desk to find Ava and her niece standing in front of the desk. "Good morning, Miss Johnston. How may I be of service?"

Her lips twitched as he said her name, but he wasn't going to be informal if she had started the exchange in a formal fashion. She could laugh at him all she wanted to.

"Miss Riley would like to be signed in for story time. Isn't that right, Peanut? You want to listen to stories and play games with the other children, don't you?"

There seemed to be a hint of uncertainty in Ava's tone as she asked the question of her niece.

Eddie sat down at the desk and pulled the registration clipboard from the drawer next to the computer. "You're the first to arrive, Miss Riley, which means you get to pick the first name badge." He placed three sheets of large animal-shaped stickers in front of Ava.

Riley stretched her neck high to peek over the top of the desk as she stood next to Ava holding her hand.

"There are bunnies and puppies and chicks." Ava lifted each sheet so that her niece could see the animals as she said the name.

"Tick-tick! Tick-tick!" A large smile spread over the youngster's face.

"Then, a chicken it is."

Eddie was happy for the translation, because he wasn't certain he would have gotten that from the exciting babbling. "Is it R-I-L-E-Y?"

"Yep, no creative spelling for this one." She bent to pick up her niece, who was trying to climb her leg.

"That makes my job easier." He printed Riley's name on the sticker with a permanent marker and then peeled it off and handed it to Ava. "You can affix that to her, and then, if you would just sign the form that says you give her permission to be in our care for an hour, you'll be all set." He glanced at the clock. "Jenna should be in the story time room in about fifteen minutes, and then, it will start filling up fairly quickly."

"We're early so we can take a walk around the library to see where everything is and to check out the toys in the kid's section for after story time – if she makes it through the whole time without me." She placed Riley back on the floor and squatted down to her level while sticking the name tag on the front of her niece's shirt." She peeked at him over the top of the desk. "It's been a rough morning." She rolled her eyes skyward and blew out a breath before standing and taking a pen from the can of them on the desk so she could sign the paper on the clipboard.

Eddie grimaced. "Sorry to hear that. But it seems she's doing fine right now."

Ava laughed. "Pray that it stays that way." She sobered as she returned the pen to the holder. "Seriously, pray that it stays that way, and she doesn't decide to test how loudly she can scream. This whole Mommy leaving her with people so she can go look at houses and drop off resumes is taking a toll."

Was her sister moving? "Aw, that has to be hard on her – and her mom and aunt."

"Yeah, it is, but we'll make it through. I think."

"You will." No one with the streak of stubbornness he had seen Ava display when arguing with him was going to not survive a few trials. "Gran is here if Riley wants to say *hi*, and Trish is on the schedule to be an extra in story time today. So, that might help." Riley knew Trish pretty well and always seemed delighted to see her whenever Ava brought Riley to the library.

"Thank you. You have been very helpful, Mr. Bennett." Her lips twitched with restrained amusement once again. "Say thank you to Mr. Bennett, Riley."

"Fank ooo."

"You are most welcome, Miss Riley. Have fun." He waved, and Riley waved in return while wearing a large smile as she toddled away with her aunt. She certainly was cute. He glanced at the clock and then towards the door. No one was entering and no one was near him. He closed his eyes for a minute as he asked God to help Riley settle into story time without any trouble.

"What are you doing?"

Eddie jumped and felt his face warm.

"Sorry," Josh said, "I thought you heard me. I need the list of books to pull for placing on hold."

"No problem. Just let me hit print on the file, and you can pick the list up from the printer." He turned his attention to the computer at his side and clicked to open the right file. "I forgot you didn't have school today. It seems strange to see you here on a Friday morning."

"I'm just happy to get the extra hours."

Josh was saving up to buy a car. Next month, he'd have his driver's license, and his dad had told him that if he didn't have any accidents or tickets between then and next year, he'd let him buy his own car and would match whatever amount Josh managed to save. Eddie had heard all about it – many times.

"And there we go." Eddie made a show of clicking the print button. "It should be waiting for you on the printer in a minute."

Josh didn't move.

"Do you need something else?"

He shook his head. "I'm still wondering what you were doing when I came up here. Your eyes were closed, and your lips were moving."

The heat that had left Eddie's face crept back. Had his lips actually been moving? That was embarrassing. "I was praying."

"Yeah?" Josh's lips tipped up on one side. "That's cool."

"It is?" Eddie had always thought others would laugh at him if they caught him praying. That was why he was always careful to do it as secretly as possible.

"Yeah. I pray, too. My friend, Mitch, at school taught me how just last month." His smile grew. "And my dad finally agreed that I can go to some youth activities at Mitch's church with him if I want. I can't go to services yet. Dad's not into the whole Jesus teaching thing – that's how he says it – but he's ok with me hanging out with kids that aren't into wild partying. He thinks it will keep me out of trouble. Mitch says that one of the guys that helps out sometimes with the activities used to be into partying, but he's not anymore. I think his name is Henry, but I don't know for sure. I haven't been to any of the activities yet so I haven't met him."

Oh, Josh had already met Henry if his friend Mitch was the kid he was thinking of. "If your friend Mitch goes to Hatfield Falls Christian Church, then, yeah, that guy's name is Henry."

"That's the church!"

"Henry's my brother, and our dad's the pastor."

"No way!" Josh's eyes were as wide as Eddie had ever seen them. "That means he's the guy that's marrying Trish, right?"

Eddie nodded. "Yep."

"Cool. I know him. Wait until I tell Mitch."

"What has Josh looking so impressed with himself?" Trish asked as she came to join Eddie at the information desk. They would need two people to get all the kids signed in for story time, since most moms didn't arrive with their children until two minutes before story time started.

"He knows Henry."

Trish laughed. "Well, that is pretty impressive."

Eddie chuckled. "If you say so."

"I do, but why is Josh so pleased to know him?"

"That's because his friend Mitch has taught him how to pray, and his dad has agreed that he can go to some youth activities at Mitch's church where one of the guys who helps out is named Henry. And now Josh can tell Mitch that he already knows Henry – and his brother and his fiancé." He shrugged. "That's pretty cool stuff when you're Josh's age." And not, Eddie guessed, one of the cool kids. Josh just didn't seem to fit the mold of "cool kid." It seemed like he fit more easily into the sort of group in which Eddie had always found himself – cool kid adjacent.

Nerdy, but not so weird that the cool kids didn't accept you, and studious, while still being personable enough for them to find your intelligence to their benefit.

"And he just dropped all this intel on you?" Trish lined up the name badge sheets – one set for Eddie and one set for herself.

"Pretty much in one breath." He handed Trish a marker and the second sign-in clipboard.

Trish laughed. "Josh was that excited about knowing Henry?"

"No, part of it was excitement over knowing how to pray."

Trish's brow furrowed. "He just started talking about praying? I mean I know the kid idolizes you, but does he always just broach unusual topics with you?"

Eddie drew and released a breath. "Not always – but sometimes. However, this time, the unusual topic came up because I was praying for Riley."

Trish's eyebrows had risen high. "Is something wrong with Riley?"

"Yes and no. I guess her mom is applying for jobs and house hunting, and being left without Mommy has been taking a toll on her."

"Ah, yeah, that makes sense. Change isn't easy for lots of people – especially little people like Riley."

He could relate to that. He wasn't exactly looking forward to moving into a new home. "Are Ava and her sister moving? I wanted to ask Ava when she mentioned the looking for houses thing but didn't want to upset Riley."

"Aw." Trish knocked his shoulder with her own. "You're such a softy."

"I am not," he protested as Trish continued without paying an ounce of attention to him.

"You cook fancy food, watch period dramas, aren't short on good looks, and have a tender heart that cares if a child is upset or not – why aren't you off the singles' market yet?"

He shrugged. "I'm just not the sort of guy who gets picked first. Never have been." He had even been born last.

Trish rubbed his shoulder. "Poor Eddie."

"I don't mind."

"Pfft. I don't believe that."

"There's not much I can do about it if I do mind."

Trish cast a wary sidelong look at him. "What about Ava? She might like a guy like you since she's into books and so are you."

He shook his head. "I don't see that happening."

"Why not?"

He looked toward the door and then, the clock. What was taking those moms so long to get here today?

"Even if we get interrupted, I'm still going to want an answer."

Eddie blew out a breath. Might as well get it over with. "We argue."

"About what?"

"I don't know. Lots of things. Books."

"Is this because she likes to read romances?"

Eddie sighed. He really *should* look into finding a job in a school library where there weren't any pushy relations allowed. "Partly." He looked around again before whispering, "I don't agree with her about happily ever afters being possible. I mean, sure a couple can be happy together, but forever and all the time?" He made a scoffing noise. "How does she not get that? She lives with her sister who's a widow – a very young widow."

Trish rolled her eyes and sighed.

"And you agree with her and Gran, don't you? You didn't before Henry."

"Okay, I'll give you that my point of view has shifted. Not all relationships are doomed to failure, and it is possible that romances are not just fairytales. And yes, it is because of your brother. He's helped me see a lot of things differently. Maybe you should talk to him about it."

"No, no, no, no," Eddie said as he shook his head. "I am not talking about this with Henry."

"Then, what about Will?"

He shook his head.

"Brandon? Or Freddie?"

He shook his head again.

"Your dad?"

He blew out a breath. "Not believing in happily ever afters is not something that requires spiritual counselling. I just don't believe in them." Finally, the front door opened, and three moms and tots entered.

"But I don't want you to be picked last and die alone," Trish whispered.

Eddie chuckled and shook his head. "I'll do my best to die with someone else."

She huffed. "That is not what I meant, and you know it."

"Hello, welcome to story time," he said as the first mom approached the desk.

"This isn't over," Trish hissed.

Yes, it is, he thought as he made out a name badge for Emily. Today, during lunch, he was going to look at the job postings with the school board.

Or... he thought as he waited for Emily's mom to sign the clipboard, he could just ask Ava out and prove to everyone that they weren't a good match. He sighed quietly. But then, he might lose his job as her editor, and he really did want to know what happened next in her series – not to mention, he had plans for the money he was earning from it. Besides, it seemed a bit like a conflict of interest or some sort of ethical error for him to date her if she was also paying him to do work for her.

And as Emily and her mom walked toward the story time room, he was back to looking for jobs at lunch time.

Chapter 6

THE DOOR TO THE story time room had been closed for five whole minutes, and Ava hadn't heard a single shriek or even a soft wail – and she had put her ear against the door just a minute ago to make sure she wasn't missing anything.

She checked the time on her phone. She had twenty-five more minutes until story time was over. Did she dare to take out her work and get some done, or was that an idea that was doomed to fail?

"I'm sure she'll be fine," Lacey said from where she sat at the front desk checking in books. "Why don't you go relax, and we'll come get you if there's an issue."

Ava pointed to an unused computer in the area where the teenagers usually played games. Four of those computers were already being used by some kids that looked like they were in grade seven or eight. "Is that computer open for thirty minutes?"

From there, she'd be able to see if someone came out of the story time room or possibly hear if Riley decided to let out a shrill shriek.

"Let me check." Lacey put the book she had in her hand aside and tapped on the computer's touch screen. "Yep, it's free. I'll put your name on it."

"Thanks." She could get some online things done. They didn't take as much concentrated focus as writing or editing did. She sat down and typed in her library card number to unlock the machine. Then, she opened the browser and navigated to her blog. A life update post might be good.

Dear Readers, she began.

No, I (once again) don't have any spectacular news about being swept off my feet by my very own prince charming to report. This Author in Search of Forever is still searching.

However, the particular prince who has caught my eye – whom I told you about in the previous update, aka Library Guy – has not yet claimed some other princess for himself, so there's hope.

She paused and glanced at the information desk to her left. There was something about Eddie that just called to her. She had said that about two other guys over the course of her life, but this time, the call was the loudest she had ever heard. It was as if God were saying that this was the guy for her, but then again, she might just be imagining the whole thing as she had the other two times. She was, after all, exceptionally good at imagining things. Her sales numbers and the number of readers subscribing to her mailing list, social media accounts, and this blog were proof of that. If only it were as easy to bring real life things into being as it was to give life to a story.

Her fingers went back to typing as she watched him and remembered how he had promised to pray for Riley earlier.

He's sweet, guys. Like two shots of chocolate and extra whipped cream in your mocha sweet. I swear kindness just seeps from his pores. A soft heart lurks under his rather uptight façade.

She paused to consider what she knew about him. He was always willing to extend a hand to help others – even when those others were an awkward teenage boy or a little girl going through a trying time in her short life.

A girl's forever certainly could be a happy one if she had a guy like that who loved her. She sighed. If only he would see her as something other than the author whom he edited for. Maybe asking him to edit for her had been a mistake. She had hoped that the close working relationship might produce some sparks between them or give them time to slowly fall in love. Once again, she was reminded that what she could arrange to happen through the implementation of a forced proximity trope in her books was not so easily arranged in real life.

Her fingers went back to typing, while her eyes stayed fixed on sweet and handsome Edmund Bennett.

Someone really needs to stop me from completely losing my heart to the guy since I'm pretty sure he'll never pick me. I've been kind of cursed that way my whole life. I don't know what it is about me, but the guys I like never seem to like me. Perhaps when I was born, my mother and father received an unwelcome gift at my baby shower like Sleeping Beauty's did. Perhaps my unfortunate curse is to always be ignored by the men of my choosing until... I don't know... something happens.

She turned her attention back to her computer screen.

Do you think I should go in search of a needle on which to prick my finger? I mean, I could really use a nap. LOL My niece is struggling with some separation issues.

You see, my sister has decided to go back to work and to sell her house as quickly as possible. As we speak, there's a plumber there fixing the constantly dripping faucet in the guest bathroom and next week, he'll come by and install the new dishwasher – one without a broken front panel. Then, there are just a couple other minor fixes and some painting that need to be completed before the house gets listed on the market.

Yep, guys, I'm probably going to be homeless for Christmas this year. *smiley face* Well, maybe not homeless. I do have some leads on places to live if my sister doesn't want to continue to house me. (And no, none of those leads include going back to live with my mom and dad. Not that I don't like them, and I'd rather live with them than on the street, but I don't know, it would feel too much like I was failing at this adult thing.)

But that doesn't really explain why I need a nap.

My niece is unsettled by all the unsettling details of her mom trying to create a new life, and she's not sleeping well, nor is she complacent about being left anywhere without Mommy – even Auntie isn't as acceptable as she used to be.

Therefore, there has been much wailing (by my niece, not me haha!) and interrupted nights of sleep. Hence the overwhelming desire to go curl up in the corner of the children's section of the library while I wait for story time to be done.

Send coffee, pillows, or at least drop your best advice for helping my niece through this tough patch in the comments. (Advice about my may-never-be-mine prince charming also welcome.)

Coffee sounded good.

She checked the clock in the lower right-hand corner of the computer screen. Seven more minutes and then she'd need to sign out and get ready to collect Riley from the story time room.

She hit post on her blog post, copied the link to it, and opened her social media scheduler so she could share it in one click to several places at once.

With that done, she closed the web browser and signed out of the computer before pulling a thermos of coffee from her bag and flipping open the top.

Taking a sip, she closed her eyes and savoured the chocolate, vanilla, and hazelnut flavour. She never drank coffee without some sort of added sweetness. It was far too bitter on its own, but paired with something like chocolate and hazelnuts, it was heavenly. Addictive even.

Opening her eyes, she watched the kids on the computers next to her. They were obviously playing together from the why'd-you-do-that's and that-was-epic's she kept hearing. Oh, to be a kid again when life was only truly complicated in her imagination. Now wasn't that a shift! Half-a-dozen years into adulthood and reality was the complicated thing while her imagination seemed truly beneficial.

Her eyes scanned the parts of the library that she could see from here and smiled as she saw Gran making her way towards her. That lady was as fun as she was loving. Ava imagined her mom would likely be as spunky at eighty as Gran was since her mom was already quite the force to be reckoned with.

"I've come to see how Riley did. I see you're sitting here alone, so I suppose that means she has survived being on her own for nearly three-quarters of an hour."

"It seems that way." Ava pushed up from her seat. "I suppose I'll know in just a few minutes if Trish and Jenna survived her."

Gran chuckled. "I doubt one little lady would take down either one of them. I've seen them work with some rather challenging kiddos." Another chuckle. This one dripping with mirth. "There was this one little boy." Her head shook slowly from side to side. "He climbed everything. And he was quick, too. That little fella gave them a run for their money – quite literally – for a few weeks until he got used to the routine."

She walked with Ava towards the story time room. A few other mothers were also moving that direction.

"I'm planning to play with Riley," Gran said.

"You are?"

"I am, and if I may, I have a couple of cookies in a container in my bag that I'd like to share when you leave."

Did the lady ever travel anywhere without some sort of baked good on hand? How did she stay so slim when she did all that baking?

"I wouldn't be opposed to a sweet treat to lure Riley away from the toys and into the car. I should've thought of that, but I didn't."

Gran waved the comment away. "You're still learning the ropes with little ones. However, if you keep doing as well as I've seen you doing, you'll be a mothering pro before your first child turns five." She chuckled. "I didn't feel like I was ready to handle being a mom with any sort of success until Amy was sixteen. Thankfully, she was a cooperative teenager, or I'd probably still not feel like I was ready."

Ava laughed. "I think you're exaggerating."

Gran tipped her head this way and that. "Perhaps a bit, but let me tell you, I'm glad I was just the grandmother and not the mother when Amy's boys were all teenagers

– especially Henry. That boy." She shook her head and smiled. "He turned out pretty great though, didn't he?"

"Indeed, he did from what I have seen and heard of him." And she had seen and heard plenty about him since his fiancé was one of her new best friends.

"I hope to be able to say the same for all of them."

Ava turned startled eyes to Gran. "You currently can't?"

Gran shook her head. "I almost can, but three of them still need to prove themselves as worthy of the title by demonstrating they can care for a wife." Her smile tipped up on one side and a touch of sadness shone in her eyes. "Well, I think Brandon has reached that level, but I'm hopeful he'll get another happier chance to prove it." She leaned towards Ava and lowered her voice. "He'll get there in time, and I'll prod him along when needed, but for now, my focus is his youngest brother."

Ava chuckled. "Yeah, mine, too, but..."

"Oh, I know. He's got some learning and growing to do. Don't give up on him too quickly. He's never made decisions or moved forward as fast as his brothers." A sigh accompanied her words. "He just needs to find his confidence."

That made Ava blink. Eddie suffered from a lack of confidence? Edmund Bennett was not utterly, one hundred percent, absolutely sure of himself? She watched him stride from the information desk as he showed someone where to find something. A lack of confidence did not seem to fit what she saw.

"He plays a good game," Gran said as if she understood what Ava was thinking. "But it's a game. He just needs a lady like you to show him that he's not as good as he thinks he is."

Ava shook her head. "But wouldn't that make his confidence worse?"

Gran shrugged. "He's putting it in the wrong place – what he can do and know instead of who he is." She didn't get to say anything further as the story time door opened and children began to be claimed by their mothers.

"Hey, Peanut," Ava said as she took Riley from Trish's arms. "Were you a good girl? Did you listen to the story and play the games?"

"She was excellent," Trish answered as Riley babbled. "I hope she gets to come next week. I'll be in there again." She rubbed Riley's back. "Thank you for coming, Riley."

"Say you're welcome," Ava prompted.

"War wow wow."

"Close enough," Trish said with a laugh. "Hey, Gran, which one are you here to pick up?"

"We've got her." She wiggled her fingers in a wave at Riley. "Are you ready to play?"

Riley's eyes grew wide, and she squirmed to get down.

"Take my hand," Gran instructed, and Riley did.

Ava walked behind them.

"It seems our prayers were answered," Eddie said as she passed him. "Miss Riley seems to be doing well."

"She is. Thank you."

"Are you moving?" he asked. "I tried to find out from Trish so I wouldn't upset Riley, but from what you said earlier it sounded like you might be?"

"I am. Ali is selling the house and hopes to be out before the new year or shortly thereafter."

"Will you be moving to wherever she does?"

"It depends on what she finds and if she wants or needs me to."

"I bet she appreciates having you around to help. Riley seems to really love her aunt."

"And your grandmother."

"Well, everyone loves Gran."

"True enough. I suppose I should go make sure she and Riley are playing nicely and that the cookies don't appear until we leave."

Eddie chuckled. "She has cookies, does she?"

"When doesn't she?"

"Also true," he agreed. "Hey, let me know if you need help when it comes to moving. If I'm available or if my brothers are, I'm sure we can form a moving crew."

"That would be wonderful, Eddie." She turned to walk away but then, Gran's words about his confidence popped into her mind and she turned back. Maybe a word of encouragement would help him. "You know, Eddie, I wish there were more guys like you. You're always so willing to help." She shrugged. "Thanks."

His eyebrows had risen high. "No, thank you. I appreciate the compliment."

She shrugged again. "You're welcome. I should go." She pointed toward the kid's section.

"Have fun." He turned to go back to the information desk, but not before giving her one of his charming smiles.

She blew out a breath. Her stupid heart needed to slow down. Earning an appreciative smile for giving a little encouragement to someone should not set it off like a frightened pony. Not even if that someone was her may-never-be-mine handsome prince.

Chapter 7

"You should've built a bigger house," Henry said as he settled onto a floor cushion next to Trish and in front of Will at Will's place that evening. "Seating capacity will soon be maxed out."

Tonight, it was Eddie's oldest brother's turn to host movie night. Normally, these sibling events were hosted by Henry, Fred, or Edmund at Henry's house since he had a large living room. Brandon and Emma were left out of the rotation since their apartments were too small for a large crowd – one which seemed to always be growing. It used to be just the six of them with Blake and Tyler or some other friend, like Esther, thrown into the mix on occasion. However, not quite a year ago, it had become the six Bennett siblings plus Trish and her brother and Lacey and her sister. Now, it seemed that Ava was to be a regular part of their group due to her friendship with Trish.

"Nah," Will replied, "it's big enough for now."

"We can always add on an enormous gathering room later," Lacey said with a laugh. "One with a playroom so Ali can join us and Riley can be entertained."

"Just Riley? Any other children we should know about?" Henry whispered to Will in a not-so-soft voice, earning himself a smack with a decorative pillow by Trish. "Hey!" he cried as he rubbed his chest and laughed.

"That was for Will and Lacey," she replied. "They weren't close enough to do it themselves."

"Will's right behind me."

She shrugged. "But he doesn't have any pillows, does he, Bennett?"

Trish often referred to Henry as Bennett. Mostly when she was playfully arguing with him.

"And perhaps neither should you." Henry tried to steal the pillow from her, but she tossed it to Ava, who was seated between her and Eddie.

Eddie shook his head. Henry looked quite pleased to have not gotten the pillow and kept his arm wrapped around Trish. A small twinge of jealousy poked at Eddie's mind. Henry had never found it challenging to be accepted – well, except when it came to Trish, but even that had ended up being how things always were for Henry. People loved him. Even Josh. Who didn't even know him.

"Did Trish tell you that there'll be a new kid attending the next youth activity?" he asked.

"Oh, no! I forgot about that," Trish said. "He's impressed that he knows who you are." She laughed and snuggled closer to Henry. "Not that I can blame him, of course."

"Of course. Who *could* blame him?" Henry kissed the side of Trish's head and then turned his attention to Eddie. "Who is he?"

"Josh – a kid that works at the library with us."

"Really?" Lacey asked. "That's great. He's a nice guy."

Eddie nodded his agreement. "Yeah, he's not bad." A bit of a tagalong at times and more than a little proficient at sneaking up on him, but friendly and eager to do his work.

"He idolizes Eddie." Trish peeked at him out of the corner of her eye.

"He does not."

"Um, yeah, he kinda does," Lacey said. "You're like his librarian hero or something."

"No, I'm not. I just happen to be one of only two guys who work at the library. It'd be weird if he wanted to hang around with you, Trish, and Jenna all the time, wouldn't it?"

"Ok, before this argument goes further," Henry interrupted, "how do you know he's coming to a youth activity? Did you invite him?"

Guilt smacked at Eddie's conscience. "No, I didn't." He wasn't Henry. Henry wasn't worried about people calling him a Bible wingnut or whatever. "He saw me praying." By accident. "And he mentioned that his friend Mitch taught him how to pray recently."

"Mitch Bailey?" Henry looked super excited by this news.

"Yeah, that's who I think he means unless there's some other Mitch in the youth group that I haven't met yet."

"Nope, we only have one Mitch." Henry shook his head and smiled. "He's been asking me about how to be bold in his faith. So, he must have taken some of my advice."

"That's awesome," Fred said.

"He also must have talked you up to Josh," Eddie added, "because he was as pumped about knowing you – tangentially as the acquaintance may be – as some teens would be about a favourite singer or actor."

Henry laughed.

"Well, I'm sure the fact that Henry's your brother helped, too," Trish teased.

"Yeah, that's not likely." No one ever counted his being a Bennett as a reason to want to know his brothers. They usually went through his brothers to get to him.

"Why not?" Ava sounded shocked. "He seems to like you, so why couldn't your being Henry's brother be a mark in Henry's favour?"

"It just isn't."

"I don't buy it. I mean, you're the first Bennett brother I met, so to me these guys are all Eddie's brothers in my mind. That's how I came to know them, and that makes you the important link." She crossed her arms and gave him that challenging look she liked to use when she was daring him to prove her wrong.

"Fine. You don't have to buy it." He wasn't going to start an argument here. He wasn't even going to continue the one she seemed willing to begin.

She huffed. "I'm right, and you know it even if you won't say it."

"I just know how it has always been." Why did she always have to be either right or proven wrong? "I'm the baby brother. Trust me. I've had enough years' experience to know that my being related to any of my brothers does not make them more popular."

Fred snorted in disbelief. "In whose world?"

"What do you mean?"

"Do you honestly think all the people who befriended me in high school and college did it because of how cool I was?"

Eddie's brow furrowed. "Yeah. You were cool, and I wasn't."

He shook his head. "Well, I might have been cool – might still be."

The rest of their brothers laughed. Fred had always thought well of himself, though not in an obnoxiously proud way.

"But, at least a few of my 'friends'..." He made air quotes around the word. "... only wanted to be my friend so they could get you to help them with their homework." He shrugged. "I couldn't get too mad at them for it. I mean, you do have a pretty smart brain."

"Seriously?" Lacey's sister Cari asked in disbelief. "I thought that sort of thing only happened in movies."

"Speaking of which..." Brandon lifted the remote. "I hate to interrupt a good intervention, but we do have *The Man from Snowy River* to watch and food to eat." He pressed play while Emma dimmed the lights.

"You didn't need to be psychoanalyzed by the whole group," he whispered when he took his place next to Eddie as the lion roared and the movie studio logo faded from the screen.

"Thanks."

"I didn't know you felt that way. I always felt something similar about being Will's little brother."

"You?" Eddie couldn't imagine Brandon being anything other than sure of himself.

He shrugged. "Yeah. I'd say we all go through it at one point or another."

"Hey, keep it down over there," Henry hissed.

"Shut up," Brandon retorted.

"Boys!" Lacey snapped. "Don't start."

"Yes, ma'am," they both answered, sending a ripple of laughter around the room.

If two of his brothers were ever going to get into a knock-down, drag-out fight, it would be Henry and Brandon. In fact, on New Year's Eve, they had nearly gotten into one right here at Will's house. Lacey and Trish had mediated that fight. Most of the people in attendance that evening hadn't noticed Henry storming off or Brandon going after him, but Eddie had. He'd still like to know what that argument was about. He suspected it had something to do with Trish.

Ava bumped him with her elbow. "Hey, sorry. I get opinionated."

"It's okay."

"No, it's not, and just so you know," she whispered as, on screen, a horse whinnied, interrupting a father and son's supper in their modest cabin, which was really little more than a shack, "I understand the whole being used for homework thing, but only in classes that required writing. Except for me, people just befriended me long enough to get my help and then cut me loose. I kind of wish they had tried to work their way to me through my sister."

There was a touch of bitterness in her tone, and for the first time since he had met her, Eddie saw a small chink in Ava's unflappably confident persona.

She leaned close to him and whispered softly. "You should try writing them into stories and killing them off. It's rather therapeutic."

He chuckled softly. "Book two?"

"You know it."

He drained the last few drops of cola from his can. "Do you want anything?" He tipped his head toward the kitchen. "I'm going to get some water."

"But the movie is starting. You can't leave now, or you won't know what's happening."

"The kitchen is just there." He pointed to the island that divided the living area from the cooking area. "I think I'll still be able to hear. So do you want something?"

"No." She gave him a push. "Hurry up. Hearing is not the same as hearing and seeing."

He chuckled. "If you say so, but I think I can still see from the kitchen."

"Oh, just go," she said with a shooing motion as the title credits began to roll.

He picked his way through the cushions and chairs filled with movie-watchers to where the drinks were resting in a plastic bin filled with ice packs to keep them somewhat cold. He put his empty can on the counter and grabbed a bottle of water and was just about to head back to his seat when the dish of fun-size candy bars – Fred's contribution to tonight's snacks – caught his eye. Ava might not think she wanted anything, but he knew she would never say *no* to chocolate, so he scooped up a handful of the sweet treats and a second bottle of water before making his way back to his place between Ava and Brandon.

"Just in case," he whispered as he placed one water bottle next to her and she shushed him. Then, he took two of the candies from his hand and stacked them next to the bottle.

"Get any for me?" Brandon's voice was teasing.

Eddie shrugged as his neck and face began to feel warm. He was thankful that the lights were low. "Sure," he replied as he handed a tiny chocolate bar to his brother.

Brandon took the candy and chuckled. "Yeah, sure, you brought this back for me."

Again, Eddie shrugged but didn't say anything. What could he say? He hadn't brought that back for Brandon. He had planned to eat it himself, but parting with it seemed a small sacrifice to pay to keep his brother from teasing him.

Brandon bumped his shoulder against Eddie's. His eyebrows flicked up and his head nodded towards Ava when Eddie looked his way.

Eddie shook his head.

Brandon didn't look convinced.

Eddie shook his head a second time just as Ava grabbed his arm and gasped, causing Brandon to chuckle softly.

"Who picked this movie?" Ava hissed.

"Lacey."

Ava brushed a tear from her cheek as she looked behind her to where Lacey sat. "I didn't peg her as the kill the father off in the first few minutes of the movie sort."

Eddie patted her hand. "If it helps, I have yet to see a movie she's selected that doesn't have a happy ending."

Ava's lips curled up the tiniest amount, and she glanced his way. "Happy endings always help."

"The ending is a happy for now," Lacey said from behind them. "But I promise it's a great movie." She passed Ava a tissue. "I cry every time I watch this part," she explained. "Trust me, the ending is worth it, and there's lots of swoony moments along the way."

Eddie rolled his eyes. *Swoony*! What a dumb word. Chivalrous or gallant would be better. Seriously better. He had yet to see any female swoon into a faint at some noble or romantic thing a hero of a book or movie had done.

Swoony! It was just another thing about romances, standing right along side happily ever afters, that just weren't based in reality.

"Could someone point out the swoony bits so I can understand what they mean?" Fred asked.

"The ladies already like you, bro," Henry answered.

"Doesn't hurt to keep improving my game," Fred shot back.

"I'll point them out," Trish said, "and maybe both of you can take notes."

"Hey!" Henry protested.

"Shhhh!" Ava snapped. "Movie?" She waved her hand towards the big screen on the wall.

"Somebody's serious about her stories," Trish teased.

"You know it," Ava replied as she scooted just a few inches ahead of everyone else.

Eddie leaned forward. "That's what makes them so good," he whispered.

She turned her head towards him. "Thanks. But seriously..." She placed a finger to her lips before returning to watching the story of a young man who was sent away from his home and couldn't return until he had earned the right to live in the Snowy River high country.

Eddie watched her place her elbows on her knees and rest her chin on her folded hands. In just a few minutes, the world could fall apart around her, and she'd not know it. He'd seen her do this before while watching movies. It was as if she left the real world and entered the one created by sets and actors. He settled back to watch both the movie and Ava while he wondered if she became as much a part of the worlds she was creating in her stories as she wrote them as she did the ones found in a film.

Chapter 8

Ava hung up her coat and stepped away from the coat-track and into the main area of Hatfield Falls Christian Church's foyer. She returned Mrs. Bennett's raised-hand wave with one of her own, but waited to move in her direction until Ali and Riley were ready.

"Hello, Ava." Mrs. Bennett greeted her before giving her a hug. It was this welcoming, motherly warmth that radiated from Eddie's mom which had made Ava certain that this would be a good church for both she and Ali when they moved. They needed a soft place to land. "What brings you to our church today?"

"Pretty sure it was a car, Mom." Henry winked at Ava as he joined his mother.

"Oh, you!" Mrs. Bennett shook her head and laughed. "That's not what I meant."

Henry stuck out his hand to Ava's sister. "Welcome to Hatfield Falls Christian Church, Ali. Trish was hoping to be here to greet you, but she overslept, so she's on her way. She wanted me to say *hi* to Riley for her." He softly grasped and shook Riley's hand. "Miss Trish says hello, Miss Riley."

Riley pulled her hand back and looked at it and then Henry in confusion.

"Oh, no! Did she miss breakfast?" Ava knew that Trish, Henry, and a group of his friends met every Sunday morning for breakfast before Sunday school at the Falls Diner.

"She did, but I picked up a muffin and a glass of juice for her."

"Muhmuh?" Riley kept her hands clasped in front of her as she eyed Henry suspiciously.

"Mmhmm," her mother replied. "Miss Trish is going to have a muhmuh just like you did."

"Oh, muffins are good, aren't they?" Mrs. Bennett asked Riley, who shrank back against her mother just a bit.

"Sorry, she's usually more outgoing, but with all the changes in our life lately, she's grown a bit timid. That's why we're here," Ali said. "I'm Ali, Ava's sister, in case you hadn't already figured that out." She laughed and Mrs. Bennett laughed along with her. "I thought if we could find a new church now, before we move, and if Riley could make a few friends here, then, the idea of moving might be more fun and less scary."

Riley shook her head and scowled. "Scawy."

"No, not scary. Fun," Ali assured her.

"Well, now, fun is something we specialize in here." Mrs. Bennett touched a finger to her lip. "I probably shouldn't tell you," she whispered, capturing Riley's attention, "but I think there are going to be puppets in Sunday school."

Riley's eyes grew round, and she smiled.

"Would you like me to take you down to the children's area?" Mrs. Bennett asked Ali.

"That would be perfect." She looked at Ava. "Do you want to come?"

"No, it's probably best if Miss Peanut only has one of us to cling to."

"Ok, then, I'll see you later?"

"Yep."

She looked around the foyer "Where?"

"Um, I was planning to attend whichever class Trish went to." Ava glanced at Henry. "If that's okay with you."

"Sure. We'll be in the young adults' class. It's just down that hall." He pointed to his right. "Second door on the left."

"I'll make sure she gets there," Mrs. Bennett assured Ava. "And we'll mark the classroom on the sign-in chart, so they know where to come find you if you're needed, which I'm sure you won't be." Mrs. Bennett continued talking as she led Ali and Riley down the hall to their left.

"All the nurseries and kids' classes are down there," Henry explained.

From the grin he wore while he said it and the way his eyes had shifted from her to the door, Ava knew that Trish had arrived before she even turned to see who had let in the gust of wind that was currently making her shiver.

"Do you want a cup of coffee or tea or a cookie or anything?" Henry asked her. "There's plenty at the welcome center. Of course, they'll still be there after Sunday school for a while before church starts."

"No. I came prepared." She pulled her thermos from the tote bag on her arm. "I'm kind of picky about what kind of coffee I drink."

He chuckled. "So, you're a coffee snob?"

"Nah, I just like it to be more chocolate than coffee most times."

"If chocolate's what you're looking for, I think there are some chocolate chip cookies on the tray today."

"Oh, tempting! You might be able to talk me into eating one of those."

"Hey." Trish was still straightening her sweater as she joined them. "I'm going to need a cookie or two this morning."

"Nope, you have a muffin and some old lady juice." Henry handed her the bag and glass he held before giving her a quick kiss in greeting. "Mom took Ali and Riley to Riley's class, so we should probably go find some seats near the door in our classroom."

That did sound like a good idea, but... "First, you need to show me where to find those cookies."

"Just over here." Henry turned to lead the way.

"What is old lady juice?" Ava asked Trish.

Trish chuckled. "Only my favourite kind."

"And that is?"

"Pink grapefruit, which, according to Henry, is a beverage for the over sixty set."

Henry held out a plate of cookies and squares to Ava. "I'd never met anyone who drank that juice who wasn't over sixty before I met Trish."

Instead of taking a cookie, Ava held out her hand to him, and he shook it while looking at her warily.

"Hello, my name is Ava, and I like pink grapefruit juice, and I'm not sixty."

He laughed.

"It's probably due to my mother's bad influence. She insisted that Ali and I have a glass every morning before we went to school." She selected two sizable chocolate chip cookies from the tray Henry held as she explained. "And now, it just doesn't seem right not to have some with my breakfast."

"Mothers, eh? They sure can be troublesome," he quipped.

"Why are we condemning mothers?" Fred asked as he filled his travel mug with coffee.

"I see you found chocolate." Eddie, who had joined them with Fred, stopped next to Ava, who drew in an inconspicuous breath through her nose. "It's good to see you here," he continued as Ava appreciated whatever it was that always made him smell so good. "Was Riley fine with being at a new place?"

Fred and Henry had stopped what they were doing and were watching her and Eddie.

Ava tried to ignore them. "I won't know until Ali shows up in class, but she seemed to be okay with things. There was no screeching in the car when we pulled into an un-familiar place, nor did she fight being taken out of her car seat."

"That's good to hear." He glanced at his brothers. Apparently, he was also uncomfortable with being watched. "I know you mentioned you were concerned about that yesterday."

"Yesterday?" Henry asked.

"At the library," Trish inserted. "Ava likes to work in the computer room across from Gran. We see a lot of each other."

"We do," Ava agreed.

"Oh, that's right. You're a writer of some sort, aren't you?" Henry said.

Ava nodded since she was in the middle of chewing chocolatey goodness. Henry knew exactly what sort of writer she was because Trish knew.

"And I assume chocolate came up at some point," he said it as if he was explaining things to himself and not asking a question.

"Something like that," Eddie muttered.

Why did Fred seem to find that answer humorous?

"Are you joining our class?" Eddie asked.

"That's the plan," Ava answered.

"Then, we should probably get going." Fred popped a small fruit square in his mouth – all of it. All at once. And then, waved at someone behind Ava. "Gran," he managed to say around the food in his mouth.

"She's already seen you, so you better go say *hi*," Trish said. "We'll wait for you."

"There's no need to wait for me. I can find the room on my own." Ava looked at Henry. "Second door on the left, right?"

"Yep."

"You go eat your breakfast and save me and Ali a couple of seats near the back."

"You don't think Riley's going to make it through Sunday school?" Eddie asked.

"It's just precautionary."

"You sure you don't mind if I go eat?" Trish's stomach rumbled as if to punctuate the question.

"It'd be nice if your stomach didn't growl like that while the teaching is happening," Ava teased.

"But I feel bad leaving you in a strange new place."

"I've been to some singles' activities here, so I know people. I think I'll be fine. I do new things on my own all the time. It's church. Remember, I don't have reasons to find church scary." She said the last bit softly, just for Trish. If she had Trish's church experiences, she might want someone to stand by her side the whole time she was meeting the members of a new congregation, but as far as she knew, there were no Mrs. Norrises who attended this church, and the people who knew what she wrote and attended this church weren't about to condemn her for it, so she felt safe.

"You really don't mind? I'm the one who suggested that you start coming here."

"I'll say *good morning* to Gran, too, if that helps?" Eddie asked Trish, who grinned in response.

"That'd be perfect."

"I can find a room all by myself," Ava protested. Trish's *perfect* sounded too enthusiastic, and she was pretty sure she knew why.

"I didn't say you couldn't," Eddie replied. "And I'm not doing this for you; I'm doing it for Trish."

Was there a reason why he looked away when he said that and his ears seemed to grow red? The hopeful part of her heart wanted to think there was and that it had to do with him liking her, while the more realistic part of her brain reminded her that this was Eddie. He liked to be helpful, and that hopeful part of her heart had a poor track record when it came to deciphering if guys liked her or not. It was too bad really. She'd rather that he had asked to stay behind because he liked to spend time with her.

"Fine. I'll let you make sure I get to the right room."

"See. That wasn't so hard, was it?" Trish asked before quickly moving away.

"Yes, yes, it was," Ava muttered to where Trish had been standing.

"I can say *hi* to Gran and then leave you to find your way on your own if you prefer," Eddie offered.

"Nah, I'm good. It's just that grin of hers. She's up to something."

Eddie chuckled. "That's just one of the reasons she and Henry make a good pair. What do you think she's up to?"

Ava cast a sidelong glance at Eddie. Should she tell him? Trish had been quite adamant yesterday that Ava should make her admiration for Eddie more obvious to him, but he had just offered to leave her. It wasn't as if he seemed all that into her – regardless of what Trish said about him watching her more than the movie on Friday night.

"Hey, Gran." Eddie gave his grandmother a hug. "Ava made it, Ali is seeing Riley settled into class, and Trish and Henry are going to save seats for us in our class – plus one for Ali."

"For you? As in both of you?" Gran's eyebrows were lifted over inquisitive eyes.

"Trish wanted to make sure I got to the right room, but she hadn't had breakfast, so I told her to go on ahead, and Eddie offered to stay with me for her while I said *hello* to you." She let the words tumble out of her mouth in a continuous and rapid string.

"And Ava thinks Trish is up to something because she was grinning when she hurried away."

Gran chuckled. "I wonder what she's up to." She shared a knowing look with Ava.

"Wait. You know what Trish is doing?" Eddie asked. "How do you know everything?"

"I don't know for sure. I just have my suspicions."

"We should probably get to class." It was probably best to stop this conversation between grandmother and grandson before Eddie could ask for more information and Gran gave it. Gran had also heard about Eddie's less than attentive movie watching.

"I hope you enjoy it."

"Thanks."

"What's Trish up to?" Eddie whispered.

"I wouldn't want to spread rumours." Her answer was met with a huff that nudged her desperate hopeful heart just enough to override her sensible brain. "However," she continued, "don't be surprised if we end up sitting next to each other." She blew out a breath. There. She had done it. She had put out in the open what was sure to slap her in the face and leave her, once again, doubting her own chances at finding a happily ever after.

"You mean she..." He wagged a finger between himself and her.

Ava nodded and attempted to breath.

"But I'm just your editor and friend."

"I know." *Friend.* Stupid word.

They had almost reached the door to the Sunday school room before either of them said anything else, and, to Ava's surprise, it was Eddie who spoke.

"I wouldn't mind sitting with you, if you don't mind it," He sounded rather nervous. It was endearing, until he continued. "I mean, you write romance, and I don't like romance, but..."

"You like my books."

He shrugged. "True." He blew out a breath. "So, you're okay with us sitting together?"

She shook her head. This was ridiculous. People over twenty shouldn't sound so much like junior highers. But here she was having an "I like you. Do you like me? Check yes or no." sort of discussion with the guy she liked. It was better to just rip the bandage off, do as Trish advised, and face the pain of rejection now rather than later.

"Yeah, I'm okay with that. In fact, I'd kind of like to know if we could be more than just author and editor friends. You're a good guy even if you don't believe in happily ever afters."

She literally saw his throat move up and down as he swallowed, and the thought that anyone knowing she liked him was so terrifying almost made her tell him to forget what she had just said. Listening to Trish and facing rejection now was maybe not the best choice. That hopeful heart of hers seemed to once again be leading her straight into heartache.

"It's just one class, and maybe she hasn't saved seats for us that are together," she offered as a way to make the idea more palatable to him.

He pulled the door open and smiled. "It probably wouldn't be too bad a thing if she did."

It wasn't a resoundingly encouraging comment, but it was enough to set some foolishly optimistic butterflies to flitting in her stomach.

"Do you think we can not argue for a whole forty-five minutes?" he asked as he took a seat next to her.

"I hear miracles still happen." And she believed it was true since the guy she had been crushing on for several months was sitting next to her and hadn't blown her off when she admitted that she liked him. If it wasn't a miracle, it was most definitely a first, that's for sure.

Chapter 9

"Do you think Emma would like this?" Fred held up a charcoal grey sweater. "It has that sort of neck on it that her other ones have. See." He held it up against himself. "The neck comes up just a little bit here but not all the way up to your chin."

"Is that the only colour in her size and that style?" Eddie turned his attention from randomly watching shoppers walking past the store in the mall to his brother.

"Nope, but I like this one, and it seems like it would match a lot of things. So do you think she'd like it?"

Eddie shrugged. How was he supposed to know? "I don't know why you don't just buy her something that she puts on her list."

Fred let out an exasperated huff. "Where's the personal touch in that?"

"It's in the getting her what she wants. Duh." Eddie preferred being certain about a gift rather than guessing. Fred thought that was too predictable.

"Oh, go look at something and stop being so Scrooge-y. She always likes my gifts."

That was true. Fred was the best at picking out gifts. Not even Brandon was as good at it as Fred was, and Brandon was pretty good.

"If you think she'll like it, then get it. If you're wrong, we'll mark it on the calendar as a special day, and then a week after Christmas, she can return it and get something on her list that she didn't get." Eddie lifted the sleeve of a soft peach sweater that he thought would look good on a particular romance novelist, and then, dropped it as quickly as the thought had entered his mind. He and Ava were only friends considering if they could be more. They were nowhere near the buy each other things because it would look good stage of their possible relationship.

"That's a great colour. Maybe I should get that instead?"

"Nah." This wasn't an Emma colour. It was an Ava one. "I think you should go with your first choice. I'm going to go to the bookstore across from here. Come get me when you're done, and then we'll go to the dollar store to get wrapping stuff and cards and candy and all that." He liked shopping for Christmas early enough to be able to buy what he wanted and not just what was left over after everyone else had decimated those aisles of the dollar store.

Fred cocked an eyebrow over a speaking look. "It's your day off. I know you like your job and all, but do you really need to go smell the books?"

"I am not going to smell the books." Eddie rolled his eyes. "I'm looking for a gift."

Fred's head tipped and his eyes lit with interest. "For who?"

"For whom."

"Ok, for whom, Mr. Persnickety Editor?"

"Ava." He ignored his brother's look of surprise and hurried toward the door. Fred would catch up with him eventually, and then, he'd have to try to explain that it was just because he was working for Ava in a convincing fashion. Trouble was, he'd never felt compelled to buy gifts for anyone else he had ever edited for. They had gotten a card and maybe a box of chocolates, and that was all. Ava would get some chocolates, of course, but there were some pens and notebooks he had seen that she might like. The current notebook that she kept her ideas in looked like it was getting full.

He stopped at a display of bookmarks that was just inside the entrance to the bookstore. A small one might be good for marking her spot in her ideas book. He smiled as his eyes landed on the exact set he should get. They were the metal kind that slipped over a page, kind of like a paperclip. One of them said, "One more chapter," while the other had "to be continued" on it.

With those in hand, he moved further into the stationary section of the store and had just picked out a set of soft touch pens, the kind with the clicky top that Ava liked to click repeatedly while she thought, and was just beginning to peruse the notebooks when Fred finally caught up with him.

"You're getting Ava a gift?"

Eddie nodded. He picked up a small notebook that matched the pens.

"Why?"

"Because I work for her?"

"Why are you asking me?"

"I'm not. It was an inflection of the voice indicating that the answer was something you should have been able to deduce." The pages of the notebook were lined. It would work.

"So it has nothing to do with you watching her watch the movie Friday night and then sitting with her in Sunday school and church yesterday?" Fred asked as they took their place in the checkout line.

"I wasn't watching her watch the movie," he lied.

"Yeah, you were. I'm pretty sure that Ava and Will are the only ones who didn't notice, and they both have people to tell them about it."

Eddie could feel his ears growing warm. He hadn't thought he had been so obvious. "She just gets so engrossed in the movie. I don't think I've ever seen anyone watch like she does. It was an oddity. That's all."

"Nope."

"I wasn't asking you to agree."

"Whether you were or not, I'm disagreeing and not allowing that to be the reason." They moved forward two places. "Maybe if you hadn't gone straight to her at church and then volunteered to stay in Trish's place and then sat next to her without complaining, then, I might believe you, though that still does leave the texting each other about chocolate."

Eddie sighed in exasperation. "I already explained the chocolate."

"You did, and I believed it at the time, but now? I'm not so sure." He bumped his shoulder against Eddie's. "You can tell me if you like her. I'm not going to tease you."

"Don't make promises you can't keep."

"I'm not."

"You are. You know as well as I do that if I tell you that I might like her, you're going to get excited like mom does and tell everyone else and/or bring it up in a teasing fashion over and over to find out what you can about how things are going." Fred was the more excitable of the two of them. In fact, he was the most excitable of all his siblings.

"You like her." Fred nodded his head and smiled. "I knew it."

"I did not say I liked her."

"Yes, you did, and if you'll notice something other than yourself, you'll see that I did not tease you or shout about it in jubilation."

"I said *if* I tell you. That's a conditional clause indicating a hypothetical situation."

"Don't grammar me. I know what I heard. I'm not a doofus."

They were at the cash register now, and Fred moved ahead to wait near the door, where he stood, watching Eddie and looking annoyed.

"I'd tell you if I had a possible crush," he grumbled when Eddie joined him. "Don't know why you don't trust me."

Ugh. Guilt settled in like a thick fog on a cold autumn morning. "Fine. I might like her. I mean, I do like her, but there are reasons for perhaps not allowing that."

"Such as?"

"I work with her. She's paying me to edit her books."

Fred nodded. "That could be tricky, but is that it?" He stood in front of him with arms folded, holding his gaze and still looking annoyed.

"She likes romance."

"Well, that's a stupid reason to not like a girl, and it's going to make it hard to find one to like. Lots of them seem to like romance. I think it's like a built-in thing that God created them with."

Eddie tipped his head towards the end of Hatfield Falls' small mall where the dollar store was, and then started walking that way. "But I've always been rather outspoken about my dislike of the genre."

"So what are you thinking? That if you like her, people will think you're stupid?"

"Yeah, something like that." There was more to it, of course. But did he dare tell Fred that secret?

"They won't. It's not like you've suddenly become a romance fanatic or something."

"Actually..." Eddie glanced at Fred and shrugged. "I might have been somewhat wrong about romances."

Fred grabbed him by the arm and pulled him towards the food court – if you could call three food service places a food court.

"This requires food and sitting," he said as he stopped at a table. "Sit. I'll get us a box of Timbits."

Eddie sat and waited while Fred joked with the girl behind the Tim Horton's counter and likely ended up with a couple extra donut holes in his box. Why couldn't twins be alike in more than looks? All his life, Fred had walked into any and every situation as though he belonged there, while Eddie had felt like an outsider more often than not.

His brother plopped the box of twenty Timbits on the table and took a seat. Then, he opened the container. "All sour cream glazed, and she tossed in a couple extra when I said I was using them to bribe you into sharing secrets."

It was just as he had expected, but Eddie wasn't complaining about getting extra Timbits, especially since sour cream glazed donuts were among his favourites.

"Now, spill." Fred demanded. "What do you mean by you might have been wrong about romances?"

Eddie took a bite of donut and chewed slowly. "You cannot tell anyone this. And I mean anyone."

"Goes without saying. Twin code activated."

"Okay, so..." He took out his phone and opened his library book reader app. Then, he turned the screen to his brother. On it were four books. All romances. All Ava's. "This is what I've been reading."

His brother took the phone from him and tapped on one and then another of the books, pausing to read the descriptions of each while Eddie ate little round donuts.

"Well... Um... And you like them?"

Eddie nodded.

"They aren't drivel – that's the word you often use when arguing with Emma about romances, right?"

"Yep, and nope, they aren't. The first one, it deals with the loss of a parent. The next one addresses the disparity between men and women in the time period. They all have something of substance at their core that the love story helps the characters navigate." He blew out a breath. "They're good. Really good. And frankly, more entertaining that any of the classics I've read. It's like watching that movie on Friday. An enjoyable way to pass the time."

"They're all by the same author, so maybe she's just a one off?" Fred offered as a way to reconcile Eddie's former opinion with the one he now held. "Have you read any other romances?"

"No, just ones by this author so when I edit her upcoming releases, I know what's already been written." His heart beat a little heavier in his chest as his brother's eyes grew wide and he looked at the screen of the phone he still held.

"Ava wrote these?" he whispered.

Eddie nodded. "But you can't tell anyone. She doesn't want readers to know her pen name."

"Did she make you sign a non-disclosure agreement?"

"No, my telling you this is not breaking a written contract."

"But you promised not to tell?"

"Yeah, so..."

"I won't say a word to anyone." He made an x over his heart. "Wow." He slid the phone across the table to Eddie. "That's actually really cool."

"You think so?" That was surprising. He had expected to be laughed at – at least, a little bit.

"Yeah. I don't know any authors – well, except for Ava but then she's not really telling what she writes so that's not like knowing an author and being able to point to one of their books. And you're editing them." He shook his head. "That's pretty impressive to me. Wow. And you know what makes it the coolest?"

"I couldn't even try to guess." He was still trying to wrap his head around the fact that his twin hadn't teased him. Not even a little.

"These books." He tapped the phone that still lay on the table. "These books must be really good, which means Ava is not just some wanna be. She's the real deal."

Eddie's eyebrows drew together in confusion. "How do you figure that?"

"You read them and just told me that were good. You know books, and you're picky. You telling me that these books are good is like Will telling me that the house is sound. Or Dad telling me that what I'm doing is fine to do and not a sin or something. It's take-it-to-the-bank truth."

"Ya think?"

"Yep. One hundred percent."

Eddie blinked and his eyebrows rose high. "You really value my opinion on books that much?" Being compared to their eldest brother or father was something. Something he had never in a million years ever expected to happen.

"I do. It's not that I agree with you on everything, but I know when you evaluate something, it's done well and from a base of knowledge of the subject."

Well, that was going to take a while to digest. He had never seen himself that way. He'd always assumed he knew what he was talking about and asserted himself as if he did, but from all the teasing he got about books from his brothers, he thought what he knew well was not something they valued. And that had often made him feel unimportant. But maybe he was wrong. Maybe he wasn't such a second-rate Bennett as he thought he was.

"Thanks."

"No problem. What are twins for? Right?" Fred picked a Timbit out of the box and popped it in his mouth. "So you like her?"

Eddie sighed. "Against my better judgement, yeah, I kinda do." Probably more than kinda.

"Then, don't let yourself talk yourself out of it." Fred gave him a pointed look before sticking another whole Timbit in his mouth.

Could he do that? He wanted to. Eddie glanced down at the screen of his phone. "I'll try."

Chapter 10

AVA STARRED AT THE information desk of the library while she began typing a blog update to her readers. It wasn't hard to type and watch Eddie. Her fingers were intimately familiar with where they needed to go to hit the right letters in the proper order. If only she knew how to navigate a relationship as deftly. Sadly, she couldn't.

Dear Readers,

Remember how I told you two weeks ago that I had told my prince charming that I liked him, and it seemed like he was okay with the notion?

Yeah, well, I may have effervesced too soon. Now things are just awkward. I show up to work, and he makes time to say hello and ask about my day. I catch his eye across the room, and he smiles. But, aside from sitting with me at church, that's it.

It appears that I am not the sort of leading lady who inspires undying and demonstrative devotion. Guess I should have had that figured out since I was the one who had to break the news to him that we should try getting to know each other outside of work.

To say I'm a bit disappointed wouldn't be a lie. I've never been good at these relationship things outside of novels...
thoughts screech to a halt

I'm going to die. Well, probably not literally, but emotionally, I might just fizzle to nothing. Sir Jerk-a-lot – remember him? The guy who I told you about who pretended to like me in high school and even suggested that we would go to prom together, but then, he took someone else just as soon as he knew he had passed English Composition and would graduate? He's here.

He just walked into the library where I am writing. I'd slide under this table if I didn't know that the sweet lady next to me would ask questions and that would likely draw more attention than just sitting with my head down would.

Gotta run and take some deep breaths while wishing to be invisible.

P.S. If you have any fairy godmothers on speed dial, can you put in an urgent request for me?

Ava scanned the blog post for any words underlined in red, and after correcting the one typo she found, hit post. Then, she slouched low in her chair and peeked over her laptop towards the information desk. Why was he here? Sir Jerk-a-lot had always been more slap shots and hat tricks than he was studious. That meant there was likely no need to worry about him even seeing her in a quiet computer work room, right?

Of course, that knowledge did nothing to calm her.

At the computer across the aisle from her, Gran clucked her tongue.

"You think he'd be smarter than that," she muttered before casting a sad smile Ava's direction.

Ava leaned to her left so she could see what was on Gran's computer screen just as that very lady closed whatever she had been doing, stood, and reached for her cane.

"You want me to trip him with this or maybe give him a good hip-check? I've got a bionic one of those, you know."

Ava blinked at Gran. "Who?"

"Take your pick. I can start with Sir Jerk-a-lot and move on to my youngest grandson." She slung her purse over her shoulder and pushed in her chair. "I was reading your update. It looked like you were writing one, so I waited to read it before I had to leave. I'm not a fan of scrolling and reading on my phone."

She didn't know Gran read her blog. She might need to be a bit more circumspect with what she shared there now that she knew. "Thanks for the offer of support, but it's probably best if you don't beat anyone up for me. It might get you banned from the library and then who would help me avoid doing my work?" They always spent a few minutes talking before settling into whatever they planned to do whenever they both ended up in the computer room – which was nearly daily.

"Well, I would hope it would be the young man up there at the info desk, but it seems he doesn't know what to do with the knowledge that a beautiful young woman likes him." She shook her head. "He's usually so bright." She sighed. "I'm sure he'll figure it out eventually. I've learned over the years that I have to have patience with Eddie. He doesn't make snap decisions. Don't give up on him just yet."

She paused and turned so that she was standing in front of Ava. "I'd really like to hear more about the other guy, but my physiotherapist might not find 'dishing about guys' to be an acceptable reason to be late to an appointment." Her head tipped. "You know my physio is single, a

Christian, and rather handsome. I mean he's no Bennett boy, but he's pretty cute."

Ava held up her hands. "One guy disaster at a time, please."

Gran chuckled. "I'm just happy to have finally found someone young, sweet, and available who isn't completely resistant to my meddling. See ya tomorrow?"

"Lord willing." That was the reply that Gran always gave Ava when she asked the same thing.

Gran tapped the tabletop in agreement and gave her a wink before heading toward the library's entrance.

Ava pulled out her ideas notebook and flipped to the page she had written on last night when she should have been sleeping. She grimaced in uncertainty as she read the notes. Would it work? Could an accident while skating bring her hero and heroine together in a way that didn't feel like the author was forcing the issue? The two main characters were awfully far apart at this moment in the story.

She clicked her pen as she thought. They were at a yuletide house party that was about to end, since Twelfth Night had just passed, so going skating was not out of the question.

"I see you still do that."

Ava's heart jump from its steady rhythmic rate of beating to trying to gallop away without her. Why would Sir Jerk-a-lot need to use a computer? And why did he have to choose Gran's computer? Every other computer in this room was currently empty. And why did Gran have to have physio today of all days?

Ava shrugged and clicked her pen. "Old habits are the hardest to break."

"It's been a while."

"Not long enough," Ava muttered. Forever would not be long enough.

His chuckle to her reply sounded a tad bit derisive. "You're not still mad at me about that misunderstanding back in high school, are you?"

Misunderstanding? There was no misunderstanding. It had been a player playing. And she had been played. She picked up her phone and clicked on her sister's number. *Remember Sam from my senior year?* she typed. *He's here. Help!*

"Something like that. Yep," she said in reply before turning her attention back to her notebook of ideas. Maybe he'd take the hint and leave her alone if she ignored him.

"That doesn't seem very *Christian* of you." The chuckle that accompanied this statement was less friendly than the first mocking one had been.

She shot him a glance. "You're right. It probably isn't." She wasn't going to fall for his use of the word Christian to manipulate her this time. "Guess I'll have to pray about it." She favoured him with a tight smile.

Her phone vibrated.

Be nice.

She drew her bottom lip between her teeth and typed *too late* in reply to Ali.

Leave.

That was probably a good idea.

Will do, she replied and then started packing up her things.

"Running away again?" Sam asked.

"I'm sorry?"

"You always were rather timid." He blew out a scornful huff. "I knew you wouldn't put up a fight if I stood you up for someone less prudish." His lips curled up on one side into that smirk which Ava had at one time found so attractive. "The play paid off. That was one memorable prom night – lots of dancing both in the gym and afterwards, if you know what I mean."

Oh, she knew what he meant. There was a reason he used the word prudish to describe her. "I'd say I feel sorry for her, but I think Amber knew exactly what she was doing when she agreed to go out with you." She shook her head. "You know, Amber, unlike some, never pretended to be what she wasn't. I suppose I can respect that about her."

"But you don't respect anything else about her?"

Ava shrugged as she jammed her laptop into her bag. She really needed to get out of here before she said something truly horrible. "I never knew her enough to know anything else about her to respect. I suppose she had some nice clothes and a good car."

"I married her."

Ava froze. "That's interesting."

"She left me for a guy that made it to the farm team instead of just the junior league." He tipped his head and stared at Ava.

Was he daring her to say what was on the tip of her tongue – that he had gotten what he deserved, that Amber truly never had pretended to be what she wasn't? Well, she wasn't going to say any of those things.

"That's too bad."

"Are you married?" he asked.

Ava blinked.

"I don't see a ring," he continued. "Are you dating anyone?"

"I really don't see why you need to know that."

He shrugged. "I've often wondered if I took the wrong girl to the prom." His brow furrowed as he looked at the screen in front of him. "Why would they want me to do that?" he muttered before shaking his head. "I just moved, and the internet isn't hooked up at my place yet." He glanced at her. "And I didn't want to use up all my data uploading a video." He connected his phone to a cord and then plugged the other end into the computer. "So, you dating anyone? If not, maybe we could go get a coffee when I finish this? It shouldn't take long."

He was asking her out? He had walked in here, made fun of her, and was now asking her out? She shook her head. It really shouldn't surprise her. That's kind of what he had always done. Not that she had recognized it at the time. She had thought he was teasing in a flirty fashion and not truly being mean. However, Ali and Frank had finally made her see the truth by the middle of summer after her final year of high school.

"I have things to do, and –" She stepped closer to where he was working and lowered her voice, "I still don't put out."

His eyes grew wide. "You're not still a v—"

"Yes, actually, I am."

His eyes swept up and down her figure, and he muttered a mild curse.

"Hey," Eddie stood just behind her. "Did Gran leave her sunglasses next to her computer?"

"I don't see them," Ava answered. She knew that Gran had put them in her purse as soon as she had arrived at her computer – before she had even turned on the screen.

"Are you leaving?" Eddie asked as he tapped out a text message – likely to Gran.

"I am."

"I'm done in ten minutes. Wait for me?"

"Ah," Sam said with a nod. "Not single."

"I beg your pardon?" Eddie said.

"I went to high school with your girlfriend," Sam answered. "And I was just asking her if she was single. She hadn't answered the question." He shot Ava a laughing look. "She did, however, turn down my offer to get coffee. Said she had things to do, so you might be out of luck, too, buddy."

"Oh, I always have time for Eddie," Ava replied. "Good luck getting that video uploaded. Hope your internet gets connected soon." Especially since then he wouldn't have a reason to come back to the library. She slipped her hand into Eddie's and turned with him to leave the computer room.

"I have to go the opposite way of the front door."

"I don't care. I'll walk wherever with you." She stepped a little closer to him. "Thank you," she whispered.

"For what?" he asked.

"Rescuing me from Sir Jerk-a-lot."

Her comment was met with a small burst of laughter. "Sir Jerk-a-lot?"

"Oh, yeah, he's a jerk. Seriously." She leaned toward Eddie so that their shoulders touched. "Remember the guy who dies in book two?" she whispered. "That's him."

"Oooh, that character wasn't nice at all."

"Neither was the guy who inspired him."

They had reached the side of the library where the door to the back room was located.

"Did he play with your heart like that character did with the heroine's heart?"

Ava shrugged and nodded. "And I was just as foolish as the heroine. I didn't know he was playing me until I had been played."

Eddie squeezed her hand. "I'm sorry he did that." He was standing in front of her and oh, so close.

"Me, too."

He glanced at the door to the back room and then back at her. "Come on. I'll sneak you out the back with me."

"Will you get in trouble?"

He shook his head. "No."

Ava laughed. "So then, it's really not sneaking, is it?"

His eyes narrowed. "Would you rather wait for me somewhere where Sir Jerk-a-lot can find you?"

"No!"

"Then, let me sneak my girlfriend..." His eyes seemed to search hers for an answer to whether it was fine to call her that or not. "... out the back door."

A smile spread across her face. She was more than fine with it.

"Are you guys dating?" Josh had just come around the end of one row of bookcases to go down the next and was carrying a stack of books. His question caused Eddie to jump.

"Sorry. Thought you saw me," Josh said with a shrug.

"You're incredibly good at startling me," Eddie commented. "And yeah, we're dating." His eyes once again questioned her to verify that what he was saying was true.

She nodded. Oh, she so wanted it to be finally true.

"Have you met Josh?" he asked.

"We've seen each other," Josh said.

"But nothing official," Ava added.

"Well, allow me to fix that. Josh, this is Ava. Ava, Josh."

"It's good to put a face with a name," Ava said. "I've heard Eddie talk about you."

The kid beamed. "You have?"

Ava nodded. "All good things," she whispered with a wink.

Josh chuckled and then, replied in a whisper, "He's pretty awesome."

"Agreed," Ava said.

"Well, gotta put these books away. See ya later, Ava."

"See ya, Josh."

Eddie pulled her toward the door.

"See, he really does idolize you," Ava whispered.

Eddie looked toward the aisle that Josh had just gone down. "Perhaps you're right."

"I am right."

Eddie huffed. "Fine. You're right."

"I do like the sound of that." Her tease elicited a chuckle from him.

"Let me put a couple of things away, grab my stuff, and sign out, and then, maybe we can talk about you coming over for dinner? It's my night to cook." He left her next to a table in the staff break room and disappeared across the hall and into another room.

Thanks for starting with your grandson. She typed into her phone. *He just asked me to have dinner with him,* she added before sending the message. Gran wouldn't get the message for a while yet since Ava knew she was probably still in her physio appointment, but surely the lady must have said something to Eddie, right?

"Why were you looking for Gran's sunglasses?" she asked him when he came back into the room.

He went to a locker and got his keys. "She said if that guy who had been talking to me went near you, I was supposed to go look for her glasses." He smiled. "Guess she knew who he was?"

"Sort of, but not completely." As much as there was written about him on her blog – which was a fair bit but not the whole story. Some parts were just too personal to share even with coded names.

He pulled on his coat, and since she had been carrying hers, she did the same. "So, can you come to dinner? Or does Ali need you?"

She took out her phone again. "She'll be okay without me, but I suppose I should let her know."

"Do you want to follow behind me, or do you want to leave your car here and get it later?"

"I'll follow behind."

He stood in front of her and waited as she finished her text. "Are you ready for this?" He motioned between them with a gloved hand. "My brothers can be horrible teases – especially Henry. There's no backing out gently from here forward."

Ah, his reluctance to do more than sit with her at church was making sense. Gran had said he took his time making decisions. "I am. Are you?"

He blew out a breath and then smiled. "I am. I think I finally am."

Chapter 11

"YOU CAN MAKE YOURSELF at home in the living room," Eddie said as he waited to take Ava's jacket. "I just need to make sure Fred knows we have company." Henry wasn't home yet, but Fred was because his car was out front and there was country music blaring from his room – which likely explained why Fred hadn't replied to his text.

"Sure. No problem." She put her shoes on the boot tray.

"Do you need slippers? I'm sure I have an extra pair of something you could wear."

"No, thanks. I'm fine. This is how I often walk around the house at Ali's, and I'm going to guess you don't have any toddlers here leaving toys and forgotten snacks lying around to be stepped on."

"You're sure?"

She nodded.

"If you need something..."

She put a hand on his arm. "Relax. I've been here before for movie night. Remember?"

He expelled a breath. "But this is different." She had come to movie nights as a friend. Tonight, she was here as his girlfriend.

"Perhaps a bit." She removed her hand from his arm and started up the few steps to the living room just as a new song started downstairs in Fred's room.

No, no, she was most certainly wrong about that. This was a lot different than her being here for movie night. He had only been somewhat intrigued by her at movie nights. Now, he was invested ... or becoming invested? He shook his head. Whatever it was, it was different now. He raced down the stairs and short hall to Fred's room.

"Did you get my message?"

Fred put his guitar down, crossed the room, and grabbed his phone from his dresser. "Um, looks like I did."

"Read it." Eddie turned and went to his room, which was just across the hall, and as he expected, Fred followed.

"She's here? Ava's here?" he whispered loudly. "Now?"

Eddie nodded as he took off his button-down shirt. "I asked her to have dinner with me – us."

Fred flopped on the bed. "Way to go, little bro." His fingers were busy tapping on his phone as Eddie pulled a t-shirt over his head.

"What are you doing?"

"Telling Henry. Or did you already do that?"

"Nope. I've only told you." He ran a hand through his hair. "Keep the pants or switch to jeans?"

"Jeans." Fred's fingers were tapping on his phone again.

"What are you doing now?"

"Just replying to Henry. Relax. I'm not going to text anyone else." He smirked. "At least not tonight." He put his phone away. "I don't want to ruin this, and I told Henry he's not allowed to either. Remember, I know how you were trying to talk yourself out of liking her."

That was true. It was only a couple of weeks ago that they had discussed his liking Ava over a box of donuts.

"So you're an official couple now?"

Eddie blew out a breath and nodded.

Fred simply looked at him as if he expected more of an answer.

"Okay, so there was this guy at the library that knows Ava from high school, and she doesn't like him, and he was talking to her, and Gran told me to go get her glasses if he talked to Ava so I did, and when I did, he called her my girlfriend, and it just all kind of clicked."

Fred laughed. "Well, that was a lot of words in one breath."

"I know. It is, but it's kind of how my brain feels right now. Somewhat jumbled." Not in a bad way, but in a 'where do I put this new information' sort of way.

"You're not questioning your decision, are you?"

"No, not at all. It's the right one. I know it is. I'm just not sure what comes after this decision."

"That's easy," Fred said as he rose from the bed. "Dinner. What are you making?"

"Chicken, potatoes, and green beans, and that's not what I mean."

"I know, but it's really that easy. No outlines are required for relationships. You guys have been friends for a few months now. Just keep doing that – you're still friends, just special friends."

His brother was right. He didn't need to know all the details of how everything would work out. He'd just keep moving forward as friends and allow his feelings for Ava to deepen along the way if they were going to deepen.

"Thanks, man. I needed that reminder. Is the dishwasher empty?"

Fred smiled sheepishly. "Nah, I forgot about that once I picked up my guitar and turned on the music. I'll go do it now. I won't be in your way for long."

"You won't be in the way." Although it would be nice to just cook and talk to Ava without an audience.

Fred chuckled. "Yeah, I will be."

Eddie grabbed a pair of woolly socks before following his twin up the stairs. The socks were just in case Ava's feet got cold – they weren't slippers but a second layer might be useful.

"Hey, Ava. It's nice to see you," Fred said.

"It's good to see you, too."

She was curled up in the corner chair, and from how she had to turn her head to see Fred, Eddie knew that she had been looking out the window. She had also pulled her long blonde hair back into a messy bun that sat at the nape of her neck. He had watched her do it more than once while at the library. He still wasn't sure how she managed to swirl and swoop her hair into the casual knot.

He crossed to where she was and put the socks he held on the table between that chair and the sofa. "In case your feet get cold," he mumbled as his ears began to burn.

She smiled and whispered, "Thanks," before turning her attention back to Fred. "Your neighbour has quite the Christmas light display going on over there, or he will have once he finishes doing whatever he's doing." She stood. "Tell me what to do." This part she addressed to Eddie. "I normally help Ali with dinner prep when I'm home. I'm not great at cooking, but I can usually follow simple direc-

tions without too many reminders to stop daydreaming."
She laughed.

"You don't cook?" Fred asked.

"Not often," she replied as she slipped her hand into
Eddie's and followed Fred to the kitchen with him. "Mom
found my mind's ability to wander annoying and often
dismissed me from the kitchen. Therefore, my skills are
mediocre at best."

Fred poked a thumb in Eddie's direction. "His are supe-
rior."

"You don't mind if people know you can't cook?" The
thought of sharing shortcomings as easily as Ava seemed
able to do was something Eddie was struggling to wrap
his mind around. He always did his best to hide imperfec-
tions.

"It's not that I can't cook. I can. Just not well."

That didn't make sense. "Aren't they the same thing?"

She shook her head. "If I do manage to cook something
without accidentally burning it because my mind was off
in some foreign land or time, it won't kill you."

Freddie laughed. "That's comforting to know."

"It still sounds like they're the same thing to me."

"Well, they're not." Her hand left his, and her arms
took their folded, prove-me-wrong position as an eyebrow
arched over a playfully challenging look.

"If you say so." Now was not the time to prove his point.
While she might look like she was open to a friendly debate, he had argued with her enough to know that friendly
was not how their interactions usually ended. He took two
aprons from the hook on the wall. "You might want this."

"I'll most definitely need that. I rather like this sweater and would hate to ruin it." She lowered her voice. "It wouldn't be the first shirt I've ruined trying to cook."

He chuckled and shook his head. Another easy admission of imperfection. He really wished he knew how to be so open about shortcomings. If he was, he might have asked her out before today. "How are you with washing potatoes?"

She laughed – it was something she seemed to do quite easily and often. "I'm pretty sure I can do that without ruining a thing. Do you want them peeled or cut?"

"Not peeled, but cut into chunks."

"I think I can manage to do that, too." She had taken a place in front of the sink as she tied her apron on. She definitely looked better in it than either Fred or Henry did. He tried to be subtle in his admiration as he took out a bowl of potatoes from the fridge and placed them next to the sink before getting out a pot.

"You can put them in here once you have them cut," he explained as he squeezed in next to her in front of the sink to fill the pot with water. It was kind of nice that she didn't step away from him. "I'll start on the chicken." He took out two cutting boards and two knives.

"All done. You two kids have fun." Fred ducked out of the room.

Ava grabbed the potato shaped scrub brush from little basket on the windowsill above the sink and started scrubbing potatoes and putting them on the cutting board he had put near her. "So, you like cooking?"

"I do. Not enough to do it everyday as a career, but it's one of my favourite after-work activities."

"What do you like about it?"

"It's quiet." He shot her a smile. "And, don't tell your mom, but it's a great activity to do while letting my mind contemplate things – just not so much that anything burns or boils over." He sliced one chicken breast in half. "I guess I also like the preciseness of it. There are detailed steps to follow so I can know if I'm doing things properly."

She had moved on from scrubbing to the cutting board. "Speaking of preciseness, how do you want these cut?" She poked the tip of the knife she held in the direction of the potatoes.

"Give me a minute, and I'll show you." He quickly finished cutting the chicken and washed his hands. "Like this." He took the knife from her and stood next to her at the cutting board. Again, she didn't move away. This closeness thing was nice. Almost as nice as holding her hand was. Both made his heart beat a little faster and his body warm. A little flutter of something flitted along his nerves, racing down his arms and through his body. After cutting one potato, he handed the knife back to her.

"Don't go anywhere. Let me do one and make sure the chef approves."

"I'm going to mash them, so as long as you're close in size so they cook evenly, we're good." Still, he stood right where he was while she had cut a potato. In fact, he'd rather just stand here and watch her cut spuds than return to preparing the chicken. "That looks good." He sighed silently and went to start the skillet heating while he dredged the chicken in flour.

The sound of Ava's knife sliding through potatoes and making a small thud sound on her board was the only thing he heard for a minute.

"Chicken is a favourite of mine," she said. "I think we have chicken nuggets – homemade ones – at least once a week. They're Riley's favourite. What kind of chicken are we having tonight?" She tossed the last of the potatoes into the pot.

"Creamy Rosemary Dijon," he replied.

"Ooh, fancy." She held the pot and had turned toward the stove. "Which burner? Mom says all cooks have their own preferred burners for various things."

"She's not wrong. Put that on the back left one."

She did and then stood at the stove watching him. "So the breading I'm familiar with. We do that for the chicken nuggets, but we usually use eggs first."

"This is just to give the chicken a bit of a nice crust." He flipped one of the breasts over and then picked up the package of fresh rosemary that lay on the counter next to the stove. "Do you know how to get the leaves off a sprig of rosemary?"

She shook her head. "Do you just pick them off?" She stepped around him to the side where the rosemary was.

"Not quite." He opened the package and handed her a sprig and then placed the bowl he wanted the leaves to fall into in front of her. "Hold it like this." He took her hand and placed the tip of the rosemary between her fingers and held them in place. "Now..." He stepped behind her so he could reach around and position her other hand properly. "Just use the fingers of your other hand to wrap around it and pull down in the opposite direction to which they grow. Like this." Guiding her hand in the proper motion was a bit awkward, but not unpleasantly so. "And put them in this bowl."

If his chicken wouldn't have burned, he might have stayed right where he was to help her with the other two sprigs, but he'd never hear the end of it if he served burnt chicken just because he found helping Ava strip rosemary leaves to be delightful.

She turned her head towards him as he stepped away. "Are you sure you don't want to make sure I do this right?" Her cheeks were a lovely pink colour.

"It's not that I don't want to." The admission made his own face feel flushed. "I just don't want to burn the chicken."

"Oh, yeah, I suppose we don't want that, do we?"

"No, we don't. Do you know how to mince garlic?"

"I can use a garlic press."

"That'll work. Let me get that out for you. We need three cloves for the chicken and four for the potatoes. I'll get the pot and cream set up so you can put the garlic for the potatoes in it."

"Ooh, fancy potatoes, too?"

"They aren't fancy."

"Anything that requires more than one pot is fancy," she refuted.

"Not to me."

"It is to me."

He stood in front of her. "You do like to argue, don't you?"

She shrugged. "Only when I'm right."

He laughed. "Only when you *think* you're right."

"I can't help it if I'm right a lot and you're just not able to see it quickly." She fluttered her eyelashes and smiled at him.

He leaned forward and placed the garlic press on the counter behind her. The action brought him close enough to nearly kiss her, and he considered it for a moment.

"The chicken is smoking," she whispered.

He jumped away from her to deal with the chicken. Thankfully, it wasn't burnt. "That's a bit browner than I was going for," he grumbled as he placed that piece on a plate where it would rest until he had the sauce ready to put it in.

"Sorry. I kind of feel like that's my fault."

He shook his head. "Don't be, but, yeah, I'm going to agree with you that it's kind of your fault."

She gasped.

"Only because," he continued, "I find you so distracting."

"Do you want me to leave the kitchen?"

"Never." The word was out of his mouth before it registered in his mind. "I like helping you learn about cooking." He dumped the rosemary leaves into the pan and stirred them. He could also see why Henry found the kitchen to be such a cozy place to be with Trish. The knowledge wasn't enough to make him suddenly become fond of walking into the kitchen and finding his brother and Trish kissing and oblivious to the world around them, but he had to admit that he could understand how it could happen much better now.

"If it helps, I've never enjoyed culinary instruction more." She laughed lightly as she peeled garlic. "Even if this..." She motioned between them. "Doesn't end in happily ever after, I'll know how to take leaves off a rosemary sprig." Her eyes were dancing with mischief when he looked at her.

"Nope, I still don't believe they exist," he said as he knew she wanted him to.

"They do," she replied as she turned back to focusing on the garlic.

"Nope," he replied.

She chuckled. "You'll see I'm right someday."

"I doubt it."

"Are you happy now?"

"Yeah."

"Even if the chicken is too brown and not perfect?"

He nodded his head and then said, "Yeah," since she wasn't looking at him to see his head bobbing up and down.

"Hmmm. Happy even when things aren't perfect." She cast a taunting look over her shoulder. "One day, you'll see I'm right."

He rolled his eyes. "I still doubt it."

She shrugged. "Of course, you do."

"I need the garlic."

"Nice change of topic," she said with a laugh as she handed him a bowl of minced garlic, which she didn't release until she had whispered, "I'm right." Then, she turned back to the final clove of garlic that needed pressing into the pot of cream.

He still wasn't sure he believed she was right, but at least, this argument over happily ever afters had been fun and had left him almost wishing they were real.

Chapter 12

"Ah! I caught you."

Ava looked behind her and then around the rest of the kitchen. "You caught me doing what?" she asked her father, who was sitting on a stool at the island and wearing all of his outdoor gear. He was probably here to clear the driveway since it had snowed some last night. Although, she hadn't heard the snowblower or the scrape of his truck's plow.

"Sneaking out," he said with a wink. "To go see your fella."

Ava turned as Ali entered the kitchen with Riley and their mom close behind. "How do you know I have a fella?" She raised an eyebrow at Ali.

"Oh, Ali told us when we called last night to see if we could take Riley for the day," her mom replied. "She also mentioned that this little princess is going to be in a Christmas program next month, so today, we're going to go shopping for a dress and shoes."

"Mom, there's a month before she needs them. She might grow," Ali cautioned.

"Do you think I've forgotten everything I know about growing girls?" Her mom tapped Riley's nose. "We're going to look and try some on today, but we won't buy them until the Black Friday sales happen. It'll be safe to get them then since I doubt this little lady is going to shoot up in two and a half weeks."

"Not that your mother will bring Riley home today without something new to wear." Their father shook his head. "She enjoys spoiling her granddaughter."

"And you don't?" Ava asked with a laugh. Both her parents seemed to have forgotten how to say *no* since Riley was born, but then, that was a grandparent's prerogative, according to her mother.

Her father shrugged. "Today is Mom's turn to wear the blame. Now, tell me about this guy you like – I believe his name is Edmund."

Ava drew a breath and sat down on the stool next to her father. She was not going to get out of the house without answering a few questions. She knew her father too well to think she could.

"Yes, his name is Edmund Bennett, but everyone calls him Eddie. He works at the library in Hatfield Falls. He currently shares a house with two of his brothers, but one of those brothers is getting married, so he and his twin Fred are going to live in a house that Fred is buying and fixing up. You know Trish, right?"

"Sure do. Lovely girl."

"She's engaged to a guy named Henry."

Her father nodded. "I seem to remember hearing that."

"Eddie is Henry's youngest brother."

"Oh! So his dad's a pastor?" her mom inserted.

"Yep."

Her dad's brow furrowed. "A PK?"

"Yes, a pastor's kid. What's wrong with that?"

He father glanced around the room as if he wasn't sure if he should answer her question with an audience. "Just say it, Dad."

"Well, you write those stories..." His words trailed off into a shrug.

"And Eddie edits them." She was certain her father's eyes couldn't grow any wider than they currently were. "He's not shouting that to the rooftops or anything. In fact, he's made me promise that I wouldn't tell anyone that he's reading romance."

"Ah, see!" Her father held up a finger. "That's what was worrying me. He's probably worried his parents will find out. Not everyone looks at what you write as a good thing." He held up a hand to keep her from protesting. "There are those of our acquaintance who have very strong opinions."

Ava blew out a breath. Boy, did she know that. "That's not why he doesn't want anyone to know."

"It's not?"

"No, his grandmother reads my books, and his mother sometimes comes to the book club I told you about."

His posture curled backwards bringing his shoulders forward as if he were flopping into a chair in disbelief. "But what about his father?"

"As far as I know, Pastor Bennett does not read my books, and he has never once attended a Book Drop meeting."

His eyes narrowed. "That's not what I meant."

"His wife reads romance, dear," her mother replied. "I'm pretty sure that means he's fine with it. Not everyone is like Mrs. Norris. Some of us have learned to use the sense the Good Lord gave us to think critically about things and realize that there is more than just one type of romance book in the world." She turned to Ava with a bright smile. "Now, I want to know if he's cute."

"Mom," Ali said. "Do you really expect Ava to date someone who isn't?"

"Well, no, but it's fun to see young people describe their loves."

"It's been one date, Mom. It's way too early to call that love – even for me. I'll have you know I've grown in that area since junior high school."

Her father chuckled. "I should hope so."

"However, I was the one to suggest that we could maybe be more than friends."

"Oh, Ava," her mother chided. "When will you learn to curb your enthusiasm and attempt to be reserved?"

"Probably never. I tried. I really did try, but the opportunity came up, and it didn't seem like he was going to take advantage of it, so I helped him out."

Now her father was scowling.

"He's cautious," she explained. "He's lived in the shadow of his four older brothers. I think he's allowed to not jump into things too quickly and end up being teased."

"Four brothers?" Her mother's question was laced with surprise.

"And one sister who is younger than him." She grabbed her father's gloved hands. "Look, Dad. I like him, and he likes me, but he's not as self-assured as you and me. Please, don't do something to scare him off. We've only had one date, and I learned how to make a yummy chicken dish in the process." She looked at her mom. "He cooks fancy stuff."

"Oh, well, Dick, that seems promising. If things should work out, Ava won't starve." Her mother laughed loudly at her own tease. "Now that you know the boy is nice, and that Ava seems happy, and since Riley is ready to go, we should probably leave before she takes her boots and coat off."

Her dad stood. "Your mom has a point. I'd still like to know more about this guy, however." He kissed the top of her head before pushing the remote start and unlock buttons on his key fob. "I'll be right behind you, Suzie. Just as soon as I finally get the reason for why this guy doesn't want anyone to know he reads my daughter's masterpieces."

Ava shook her head. "A minute ago, it sounded like you wished I didn't write what I do. And now, suddenly, they're masterpieces?"

"They were before, too. I was just worried about someone treating you poorly."

That was her dad – the sometimes over-protector of his daughters. She stood, wrapped her arm around her father's, and pointed him towards the backdoor. "Eddie doesn't want anyone to know he reads romance because he's always thought that romance was..." She paused. How was she supposed to say this without making her dad want to have a stern talk with Eddie? "He's an English major."

Her dad's head bobbed up and down as if he understood what she was trying to say.

"And he's had some strong opinions that he has voiced about genre fiction in the past." They were almost to the door. "And he doesn't believe in happily ever afters. He says they don't exist because no one is happy all the time."

"He believes in staying married once he's married, I hope."

"Oh, yes. He definitely does." Or she thought he did from the things he had said in his editorial notes and in their conversations. However, they had never actually discussed it.

"Works at the library, does he?"

"Daaaaad."

"Oh, I'm not going to show up and quiz him. At least, not today." He took her face between his hands. "If anyone can make him believe in happily ever afters, it's you, honey." He gave her forehead a kiss and waved to Ali before ducking out the door.

Ava spun towards her sister. "You told them?"

"What was I supposed to say when they asked where you were?"

"Dinner with friends?"

"That's basically what I said. I just might have used the word *boy* before the word *friend*."

"Do you remember any of how they were when Frank decided to date you?"

Her sister smiled though her eyes grew sad. "I remember it all. And it only seems fair that you have to go through the Dad Approval Test, too." She put an arm around Ava's shoulders. "You didn't tell me he was your editor. That's interesting and convenient for having to talk to each other a lot."

"It was one of the reasons I decided to ask him if he would edit for me – but don't tell Dad or Mom that!"

Ali laughed. "I know you're in a rush to get to the library to write." She put air quotes around the word write. "But, since I was in bed when you got home last night and Riley is with Mom and Dad, I'm not planning to let you leave without telling me about your encounter with Sam, and you haven't told me the details you won't tell Mom and Dad about your dinner with Eddie. So, go sit down at the table. I'll bring pastries and hot chocolate."

"Fine. But I'm only complying because I love your hot chocolate." Her sister had made a mix that had a touch of spice and cinnamon in it. "Say, do you have the recipe for that mix you make?"

"I do. Why?"

Ava shrugged. "I thought that Eddie might like some of it and that, maybe, I could make it and put it in a cool container to give to him for Christmas. Oh, and by the way, we're sitting at the island."

"Ooh, making him a present. That's a new one for you."

Yeah, there was a lot that was new for her about the whole thing with Eddie. "I might have lied to Dad."

Her sister rolled her eyes and shook her head. "You love him, do you?"

"Maybe? But I shouldn't. He's cautious, and I don't know if he'll stay with me."

Ali put the electric kettle on its base and turned it on. "Hey, Sam and his friends were jerks. I don't think a guy that seems as nice as Eddie is going to ask you out and then stand you up while telling all his friends about how you're too scared to round all the bases." She gave Ava a sympathetic look. "And you're lucky Dad never heard about that last part and only knows about the standing you up part."

No truer words had ever been spoken. As it was, her mother had had quite the time convincing her father that he should not storm into the school gym and demand that

Sam explain himself for not showing up to pick up Ava. Instead, her father had gone to the store and come back with what looked like the contents of the entire checkout candy counter – or at least all the chocolate from it.

"You will always be his baby, you know," Ali added. "I mean, he dotes on me, too, but not like he does you. You and he have something special."

"That's only because I wasn't afraid to put a worm on a hook and was willing to sit in an ice tent with a little heater for hours at a time." Not that she ever caught anything. Mostly, she had just written things in her notebook and discussed with her father all the ways that an ice fishing trip could go either very right or terribly wrong. He preferred thrillers and action movies to romance novels, but he could fabricate a mean fairytale when he was bouncing a line through a little hole trying to attract dinner.

Her sister placed a box of cinnamon buns in front of her. "I got these from Eddie's sister's café, *The Baked Apple*." She leaned forward and whispered, "They're better than Mom's."

"Seriously?"

Ali nodded. "I know. I didn't think it was possible either." She took one out of the box. "I'm in favour of you marrying Eddie just to have a tie to a supply of these." She took a bite and closed her eyes. "Mmmm. So good." She put the cinnamon bun on a plate and started to get their cups set up for chocolate. "Before you satisfy my curiosity about your date with Eddie, I think it's my sisterly duty to warn you that because you and Dad have your thing, Eddie might be in trouble when it comes to the Dad Approval Test." She grimaced. "You're his baby."

Ava sighed. "I suppose you're right." Oh! These cinnamon buns were something better than delicious. "Are there apples in here?"

"Yep, but the plain variety is just as good. Now, about Eddie," she prompted.

Ava tipped her head and smiled. "Do you think it would help him pass the Dad test if I told Dad that he saved me from Sam yesterday?"

"Are you kidding? A guy who rescued his baby from the horrible guy who broke her heart?" She pffted. "Definitely."

Chapter 13

Eddie peeked out the door to the backroom of the library.

"Looking for someone?"

The door thumped off Eddie's shoulder. He was going to have to start looking between those bookshelves to his left before looking anywhere else when spying out this door. Either that, or he was going to have to start wearing shoulder pads.

"Sorry," Josh said.

"Do you ever take breaks anywhere else?"

The kid shrugged. "Sometimes I actually sit in the staff room, but it feels funny, ya know? Like I'm not supposed to be there – kinda like the teacher's room at school when one of them asks you to go get something from it."

Eddie remembered being sent to fetch this or that for teachers quite often. Apparently, being studious and quiet made teachers willing to trust him with things they wouldn't have asked others to do. "I know the feeling, but we're not teachers. We're fellow employees."

Josh shrugged again. "Yeah, but you're not kids except for Kat, and we rarely work together and when we do, we don't get breaks at the same time."

"I'm still just a fellow employee." He grinned at Josh. "Even if I'm old."

"I didn't say you were old!"

Eddie chuckled. "Not exactly, but the implication was there."

"Sorry."

"Don't worry about it. I guess I'm not actually a kid anymore and haven't been one for what? Six years?"

"I don't know. I'm not sure how old you are."

"Twenty-four." Eddie leaned against one of the bookshelves that Josh was standing between.

Josh did a quick tap of each finger on his right hand with his thumb. "Ah, yeah, then I'd say six since they tend to kick us out of the house and into the real world at eighteen. At least, that's what my dad says he plans to do with me." A grin split the young man's face. "He's joking. He'd let me stay with him after that as long as I help out with things around the place – I mean more than I do now. He did the same with my older sister. She still lives at home. Pays a bit of rent and does the cooking and stuff like she did when she was in high school." He shifted to switch which foot was crossed on top of the other. "So, were you looking for someone?"

Eddie nodded. "Ava."

"She's here, but I heard her telling your grandmother that she's not going to be able to stay too much longer. It was something about needing to do some shopping for a gift she wants to make." He held up a hand when Eddie looked at him in surprise. "I wasn't eavesdropping. I was putting books away and my ears work."

Eddie laughed. "I'm going to have to remember that explanation for when one of my brothers accuses me of listening to things that I shouldn't hear."

"Does it happen often?"

"Not so much anymore, but when we were little? Yep. I tend to pay attention too easily sometimes. I mean, it's not like I try to do it. It just happens."

"I know! Same! Must be the way our brains work. That's what Dad always says."

"He's probably right." He'd like to meet Josh's dad sometime. He sounded like a decent father.

"So, you really like her, huh?"

Eddie nodded his head. "I do."

"She's pretty and nice." Josh had said that before.

"She is." His brow furrowed. "But that's not all there is to it. However, I can't quite put my finger on what else it is that I like about her. Unless it's how she's always so confident." He shrugged. "Or so it seems to me." Aside from that one moment during the movie at Will's, he hadn't noticed any unsureness about Ava. That being said, he knew from experience that a lack of confidence could be hidden behind a well-crafted façade.

"You'll figure it out," Josh said. "You're pretty smart, or they wouldn't let you do the things you do back there." He nodded to the back room and then straightened as his watch beeped, indicating, no doubt, that his break was over. "When do you leave today?"

"Six." In an hour and a half. Not that he was counting or anything. It was just one of those days when being at work was not where he wanted to be. Of course, that might be because he had been in the back room most of the time, instead of out at the front desks where he could see Ava.

Josh stopped two steps away from Eddie and turned towards him. His face looked a little flushed. "Eddie."

"Yeah."

"Um, I was wondering." He blew out a noticeable breath. "When you figure out what it is that you like about Ava, will you tell me?" He shook his head. "It's not that I want to know all the details of your life or anything. I promise I'm not being nosey, but my sister and my dad don't do things the church way, and there's this girl at school." He rubbed the back of his neck. "I'd like to maybe ask her out, but..." He shrugged. "I don't know exactly how to think about things like that in a church way. I guess I could ask your brother at one of the youth activities, but he's... Well, he's not like us if you know what I mean."

"Henry doesn't struggle much with knowing who he is, if that's what you mean."

Josh nodded. "He fits in too easily."

"He sure does."

"So, will you help me?"

Eddie sighed. While he was happy to be chosen over Henry, he wasn't excited to have to admit a deficit to the kid who seemed to look up to him. "I can try, but honestly, I haven't really been on too many dates. I've gone out with a couple of girls, but only once with either of them."

"Seriously?" Josh's eyes were wide. "But you're kinda good looking and seem to have things together – which I know sounds weird for me to say."

It might sound weird to someone else, but Eddie totally understood what the kid was saying. He looked a whole lot surer of himself on the outside than he felt on the inside. "I'm afraid some of that is just smoke and mirrors, hiding the real me. Where are you headed?"

"The 900s. I need to check for strays and dust shelves."

Well, that wasn't far. "I'll join you while you get started. Do you need to get anything?"

"Nope. I tucked my duster in between some books on the top shelf."

"As you've guessed," Eddie said as he followed Josh the few feet from the reference books to the section he was supposed to tidy, "I'm what most in high school would call a nerd. I like books. I like learning. I even studied English in college. I can play the piano. And while I'm capable of holding my own in a game of soccer, basketball, or hockey – because I had brothers who made it necessary to learn – I've never been on a sports team. I was in other less-cool activities like choir. Every one of my brothers out-shines me at something, and I'm the youngest."

Josh pulled his duster from its hiding spot and started running his finger along the numbers while he checked for books that were out of place. "That's a lot of stuff to overcome."

The right side of Eddie's mouth tipped into a half-grin on its own. It figured that it would be an awk-ward, not-yet-grown-into-all-his-limbs, high schooler who would understand him without questioning or pointing out something that was good about him as if trying to argue away his feelings of insecurity.

"You'd think I would have grown out of it, and I guess I have to a point."

"But it's kinda who you know yourself as." Josh pulled a book from the shelf and put it on the empty shelving cart he had brought to the section for that purpose. "Guess I'm stuck then? Am I always going to feel like I almost fit but never quite do?"

"Nah, I don't think so. Are you a perfectionist?"

"Not really. I mean I like things done the right way, but I don't get mad at my little brother too often when he leaves my stuff in the wrong place."

Eddie chuckled. "See, then, we're different in that way. I think that's what has kept me from shaking off the high school stuff. I keep finding things that I think I need to fix about myself. My twin, Fred, assures me that I don't need to fix anything. But I feel like I do."

He had never told anyone except for his college friend Pete, who now lived in Victoria, this much about how he struggled with things. Not even Gran had managed to wrangle this much from him. He was pretty sure that she knew all of it anyway. There was no hiding anything from her. And he had talked to his dad about it some. But no one else, except, now, Josh. It was likely how this kid feared for his future that made Eddie want to bare his soul. Perhaps he could help Josh avoid some of his own pitfalls.

"Why do you hide who you are? It's the way God made you, right?" Josh was looking perplexed and thoughtful. He was likely trying to reconcile things he had just learned at youth group with what Eddie was telling him and his own identity as a not-quite-cool kid.

"I've heard my dad say that many, many times." He took the book Josh held and put it on the shelving cart for him. "I guess it's about time I start listening – even if it is hard to believe that who I am on the inside is acceptable. I mean, I never really felt like who I was fit."

"If it helps, I don't think there's anything wrong with you," Josh said. "I don't know you really well or anything, but you seem pretty awesome to me, and except for the feeling like you don't fit thing..." He shot Eddie a grin. "I'd be happy to be like you. Cool job – yeah, I'm a nerd. Pretty girlfriend. Awesome family – the parts that I've met." He shrugged. "You got a lot going for you."

Eddie let Josh's words settle into his mind. It was refreshing to hear someone, who wasn't trying to cajole him out of a mood or into something he didn't want to do, share how they saw him. "I like seeing me through your eyes." He'd have to keep this image of himself in mind. "And, I'd say you've got a lot going for you, too. You're confident and smart, and all the sixth-grade girls in homework help time like you."

Josh laughed out loud.

"I know. They're way too young, but you do have a fan club," Eddie said as he chuckled along with Josh. "Seriously, you seem to know what you want to do, and you do it. I find that admirable. You've got great potential. In another nine years, you could have my job."

"I'd like that actually." The kid was smiling from ear to ear as he bent to dust the lower shelves and check the numbers on the spines. "So back to my question. Do you think you could help me with girl stuff? You know, doing things the church way and all? I mean you have gone to church. I haven't. And you do have a girlfriend now."

Eddie tipped his head. "I might not know enough."

"Please. You know more than me, and if I learn some stuff elsewhere, I can share it with you."

"I suppose I can help as I'm able." And he could always ask his dad if he got stuck on something.

Josh crumpled downward as if a heavy burden had been lifted from his shoulders. "Thanks, Eddie. I don't know anyone else – not even Mitch – that I'd want to talk to about this stuff."

That was something! To be trusted for advice even more than a close friend was no small thing. He hoped he could live up to the kid's expectations. "Well, I suppose I should go see if Ava is still here."

"Why don't you just text her?"

"I didn't want to look too desperate to see her." Even though he was.

"I don't think she'd think it was desperate. I think she'd think it was sweet – that's the word my sister always uses when her boyfriend does something thoughtful."

"See," Eddie said before he left Josh to his work. "I bet I'm going to learn more from you than you will from me."

"I doubt it," Josh called after him.

Eddie didn't. He'd never been great at interacting with females who weren't his relations. It was as if Fred had gotten all those genes when they were developing in utero. Fred had never had any trouble talking to girls. In fact, his best friend since they were in elementary school was a girl.

Ava was watching the door to the computer room when he entered and smiled when she saw him. He drew in a breath and released it as a sense of rightness encircled him. He was beginning to understand how both Will and Henry had found themselves engaged so quickly after they started dating Lacey and Trish. It was as if a missing piece to this puzzle called life had been found, and it fit perfectly. He made a mental note to share that with Josh at some point.

"Hi. Were you leaving?" Her bag was packed.

She nodded. "I was, but I had hoped to see you before I left."

Eddie darted a look at his grandmother who was smiling broadly as she attempted to look like she wasn't paying attention to what was happening next to her.

"I'm glad I caught you. I've been working in the back today. A new order of books arrived, and they need processing." He tipped his head toward the door. "I can walk you out. I'm on my break."

"I'd like that."

He took her bag off the chair as she rose.

"I can carry that."

He shook his head. "Nope. Absolutely not. Gran might be pretending not to notice anything, but if I were to let you carry your own bag..." He shook his head. "I'd have a complaint lodged against me."

Ava laughed. "With who?"

"With whom," he corrected and earned himself a swat to his arm. "With my mother."

Ava turned back towards Gran. "You tattle on your grandsons?"

"Only when necessary and if it's not a secret."

Ava shook her head. "Remind me to never introduce you to my parents."

Gran's laugh followed them out of the computer room.

"I thought I wasn't going to get to see you," Ava said. "It would have been a far less perfect day of work if I hadn't."

It seemed he wasn't the only one who felt desperate. "I felt the same way."

"I actually came looking for you, but you were talking to Josh." She bit her lip. "I only heard a bit of what was said before I scooted back to my work spot."

His heart sped up. "Which part?" Hopefully not the part about how he was a nerd and didn't know much about relationships.

"The part when he said he'd rather talk to you about girl stuff than with his friend, and I'm kind of dying to know what you and he were talking about and if it had to do with me or not. But," she added quickly, "I know it's private stuff so I won't pressure you to tell me or anything."

"He likes a girl at school and wants to act on that fact in a way that God would approve of, and he thinks I can give him some advice since I have a girlfriend." She was watching him closely as he spoke. "What?"

She smiled. "I think he made a good choice."

He pushed open the library door and let her enter the building's entryway ahead of him. "I've never had a girl-friend before." How many times was he going to have to admit his failings today?

"I've never had a boyfriend before, and I still think he made a good choice. You've got a kind heart, Eddie. You wouldn't steer Josh wrong. I bet you'd tell him if you didn't know the answer, or you'd put on your information desk hat and find him someone who did have the answer."

He shook his head. "You seem to think rather highly of me."

"Shouldn't I? Am I mistaken to think about you as a good guy who cares about others?"

"Well, no."

"Then, stop being surprised. You're a good guy."

"But I'm kind of a nerd."

"I like nerds. Especially the cute ones that like books." She kissed him on the cheek. It was a delightful surprise.

"By the way, my dad wants to meet you sometime, and he might show up here since he knows you work here."

"Should I be concerned about that?" He felt like he should be, and her grimace told him he was right.

"Maybe a little. I'm kind of his favourite."

Whew, that was unsettling.

"You'll be fine," she assured him. "I just didn't want him to blindside you completely." She put on her gloves. "Now, I have to stop at Friendly's before I go home, so I should get going even if I'd rather stay here. I think Mom and Dad are eating with us tonight. They took Riley shopping so it makes sense that they would eat with us before going home." She looked at Eddie with another grimace. "Don't tell Dad I kissed you, 'kay?"

Eddie laughed. "Why would I do that?"

She shrugged and smiled. "I didn't really think you would, but I needed to make sure." She peeked around them. "You know I wouldn't tell him if you kissed me either," she whispered and then tilted her cheek towards him so he could kiss it. And he did. "We should probably leave any other kind of kissing to somewhere that isn't the library entryway and for a time when you're not at work." Her cheeks were glowing red as she shook her head. "I'm entirely too Lydia Bennet-like at times."

To be honest, he didn't mind that she was assertive about some things – such as letting him know she'd like to be kissed. He would have been debating with himself for days if not longer about such things. He kissed her cheek again – it was as hot as it looked. "Just don't run away with any ne'er-do-wells, okay?"

"I promise," she said as she took her bag from him. "See you tomorrow?"

He nodded. "Call you tonight?"

"After eight," she said as she started down the steps to the front door.

Chapter 14

Rows of storage containers lined the shelves in the section of the store where Ava was standing. Some of the containers stood proudly at the edge of the shelf with a full row of companions behind them. Others had yet to be pulled to the front after one or two of their lot had been chosen to find a new home somewhere other than here, at Friendly's.

"Do you like chocolate?" Ava asked a clear hard plastic jar with a black lid as she took it from the shelf and popped open its airtight lid. "It looks like you could hold two or three cups of powder." She replaced the lid and found the container's capacity on the bottom of the label. "I knew it. You're just the right size, but you still haven't told me if you like chocolate."

Someone behind her chuckled. "I see you still talk to inanimate objects."

Ava knew that voice! Not that she expected to hear it unless she was on the phone or in Edmonton. Quickly, she put the jar in her basket at her feet and turned. "Nikki? When did you get home? I thought you weren't coming until the week before Christmas."

Her best friend since grade three grinned. "I lied. I just got here yesterday, and I didn't plan to spring my surprise on you until tomorrow. But then, I noticed the crazy lady talking to storage containers and couldn't resist." She wrapped Ava in a hug. "I'm home to stay," she whispered.

"You're what?"

"I'm home to stay. I got offered a job in Halifax, and I just couldn't pass it up. I missed home."

Ava shook her head. The last time she had talked to Nikki, she had been set on marrying the guy she had just started dating and was telling Ava all about which schools would be the best for their kids. "Did what's-his-name dump you?"

"You mean Joe?"

"Yeah, and I remembered his name. I just wasn't sure if I should use it or not." Normally, the name of any guy who had dumped Nikki was relegated to a "shall not be spoken" list – at least for a while.

"You can use it, and no, he didn't really dump me. I took a job, and he decided to let me. It just wasn't supposed to be." She blew out a breath and gave a half smile. "It was a mutual and amicable decision."

"You're still friends?"

Nikki shrugged. "I suppose, though I doubt he'll be calling to check on me. In fact, I'd be surprised if I even get a text from him ever again."

"So what you're saying is that he didn't even try to stop you from leaving which means he was less into you than you were into him, but you don't like conflict, and that means you said goodbye and left it at 'friends' because it was easier."

Nikki shrugged. "Something exactly like that."

"Well, he's an idiot."

Her friend smiled. "See, this is what I needed. My friends in Edmonton are still hoping for a reconciliation of some sort. They don't get me like you do."

"They haven't had you for a friend for sixteen years."

"They haven't, but it didn't take you more than three years to figure me out."

"But you forget. I, my friend, am a great discerner of character unless you're a hot hockey player – and I do mean player." She shook herself and tried to rein in the big cheesy grin she was wearing. "I'm so happy to see you. Are you planning to get a place in Halifax?"

"Oh, no! I'm not a city girl. Edmonton taught me that. So, I'm looking around here – maybe Wilson's Crossing – probably not further away from the city than that though."

"Are you buying or renting?" Ava knew the kind of money Nikki made and the way she liked to keep it rather than spend it.

"Absolutely buying. I've done my time lining the pockets of landlords. I think I'd like to buy something this time."

"Ali is selling her house."

Nikki blinked. "No way. She is?"

Ava nodded. Nikki adored Ali's house.

"Because of Frank?"

"Yeah."

"Do you think she'd hate it if I were to buy it? I mean, if she visited me, it could be awkward for her." Her brow furrowed. "It might be awkward for me since I know them both, and I'd be living in their place."

"It was just an option," Ava assured her. "I'm not trying to force you into anything."

"Where will you be living when she moves?"

"I don't know. Maybe with her if she has room, but if not, I have a few offers of places to stay, at least for a while, and I know Mom and Dad would be okay with me coming home until I found a place."

"Yeah, we all know you're not going back home." Nikki laughed.

"It's not a bad place."

"No, it's lovely and your parents are great. But I know you. You'd rather not have your mom in your business."

"Or my dad."

"Well, yeah, but he's not going to insist on making you learn how to cook, nor is he going to tell you how you'd look better if you put your hair up."

"No, but he might insist on interrogating any guy who took me out." She pulled her lower lip between her teeth.

Nikki's eyebrows rose. "Did Library Guy finally do more than sit with you at church? I haven't seen any updates on your blog."

"I haven't had time to write a post yet, but yes! Just after I posted that I was about to give up on him, he made me dinner yesterday." She grabbed Nikki's arm and made a little squee sound that made her friend laugh. "Actually, I helped him make dinner, and we ate it with two of his brothers, but I'm still counting it as a first date."

"He cooks?"

"Oh, yeah. And they're recipes with pretty names."

"That sounds promising."

"That's what Mom said when she found out. Dad plans to track him down to decide if he approves or not."

"Ah." Nikki nodded knowingly. "So, the reasons for not living at home are nonfictional."

"Yep." Very nonfictional.

"Well, I can tell we have a lot to discuss, but my ice cream is going to be soup soon so I should go get all the other essentials that leaving a part of one's heart behind requires."

Ava gave Nikki a hug. "I'm sorry. You're better than he deserves if he's too stupid to see how great you are."

"Thanks."

Ava didn't really want this reunion to end but there was Nikki's ice cream and her special project that required the chocolate-loving jar in her basket to consider. "I suppose I need to get home so I can try making this hot chocolate recipe without messing it up and try it out on my parents when they stay for dinner."

"I'm pretty sure not even you could mess up hot chocolate," Nikki said with a laugh.

"You'd be surprised."

"No, actually, now that I think about it, I remember a few rather crispy frozen pizzas and burnt pasta. You're right. You should go practise, but first, let's make plans to meet up and catch up."

"I'd like that." So much. "Maybe we could go to the Falls Diner for dinner tomorrow – oh, wait! I have book club tomorrow."

"Book club? The one you've mentioned to me? Is it exclusive?" Nikki's tone carried a hint of excitement. If the dictionary used pictures to describe terms, Nikki's would be next to bookworm. She read more than Ava did. Of course, writing tended to cut into reading time, so that was going to be her excuse if pushed on the topic.

"Yeah, that's the one, and no, it's not."

"So I could come?"

"Oh, sure. That'd be so much fun it you did. We could meet for dinner and then go together."

"I'd like that. And you said they don't all read the same book at your book club, right?"

"Nope, you can talk about whatever book you'd like."

"Well, then, it's a date. Five o'clock at the diner and then off to book club." She clapped her hands softly. "I can't wait for a hot turkey sandwich and to meet all the people you've told me about and hear more about Library Guy."

Ava chuckled. "You can call him Eddie."

"I know, but Library Guy is more fun. See ya tomorrow."

"See ya." Ava picked up the basket of groceries. "Alright, Mr. Jar-with-the-black-hat, are you ready to help me make hot chocolate?" She looked over her list and the items in her basket. "Cocoa. Right. I knew there was one more thing to get."

She had seen a can of cocoa like her mom always used in the baking aisle where she had gotten the spices, but she had hoped to find something a bit fancier in the organics section. This gift needed to be special. She didn't want to give Eddie anything ordinary.

She turned the corner to go down the aisle she needed. "Esther?" It seemed that today was the day to see all sorts of people she knew at the store. She had started by chatting with Blake – one of Henry's friends – at the deli counter where she was picking up a sandwich for tomorrow's lunch. Then, she had seen a couple she had recognized from the Hatfield Falls church and waved to them. Then, Nikki had surprised her and now, here was Esther.

"Oh, hi, Ava," Esther greeted her enthusiastically much like Ava had seen her do with her students when she saw them at church. "I'm just trying to decide what kind of coffee to get for a gift. I know we've still got over a month until Christmas, but once December gets here, I'll be running flat out to get everything done before winter break."

"Yeah? Do you have lots of things going on at school?"

She laughed. "Always. But this year, I get to run the holiday concert."

"Get to? Not have to?"

Esther nodded and smiled. "I've been wanting to try my hand at it ever since I helped with a spring play during my first teaching practicum. I always loved being part of productions in school – usually painting props and printing programs and such with an occasional acting or musical role to play – but overseeing the entire production was exhilarating."

"You enjoyed that?"

"Oh yes! I still do. It's why I joined the worship team at church."

"I used to help with the audio-video at my old church. In the back. Not on stage."

"You should ask about being part of the team at our church. I bet you're good at it. You tend to watch what's going on closely."

"I do?"

Esther nodded. "Unless Eddie's around." Her smile turned slightly teasing. "But then, I can't blame you. He's cute and a really nice guy. I've known him since I was ten."

"I think I'd heard you were friends with him and Fred in elementary school."

"That's who this gift is for – Fred. We've been besties forever."

Ava lifted her basket of goods. "This, if I get it right, is for Eddie."

"Ooh, what is it?" Esther peeked into Ava's basket.

"My sister has a spiced hot chocolate recipe that I love, and since Eddie likes to cook, I thought I'd try making it for him."

"Aaaawww, that's so sweet. He'll love it."

"I hope so."

"Does this mean that things have moved beyond just sitting together in church?"

"He let me help him cook dinner last night."

"Oh, that's promising. I don't know if I've ever heard of him letting anyone help him cook before. He's a bit of a perfectionist. But then, knowing his brothers, they would just torment him if they were allowed to help him. So maybe that's why. Although, I'd rather like to think it's because he thinks you're special."

"Me, too," Ava replied with a laugh.

"So, you really like him?"

Ava nodded. "I do."

"I'm glad. I think you and he make a good pair. Now, do you know anything about coffee?"

"I know it goes great with chocolate, but other than that? Sorry, I don't. You don't know what kind of coffee Fred likes?"

Her head bobbed from side to side. "I do, but I didn't want to get him the same old kind he always gets. Christmas gifts should be special, right?"

Ava agreed with that. "How about this Grizzly Claw one? It says it has a chocolatey taste. Or maybe this 454 Horse Power one since he works with cars?"

Again, Esther's head was bobbing indecisively from side to side. "Those are both good choices. You know what? I'm just going to get both. I mean, they're two dollars off right now, so... it really wouldn't be too extravagant, right?"

"Not at all."

She put both bags in her cart. "Are you looking for a good cocoa?"

"I am."

"Then, get this one. I know it's the store brand, but I've always found it to be a good one. It makes fantastic brownies."

"Then, I'll take it." Ava checked her list. "I think that's it."

"Self checkout or regular?" Esther nodded towards the front of the store.

Ava checked the time on her phone. Wow! It certainly had taken her a lot longer to pick up a few items than she thought it would. "Whichever one is moving fastest."

Esther chuckled. "Same. My stomach has been growling since dismissal time, and I'm trying not to eat between meals. It's not a diet. It's just a self discipline challenge – and only for this week and not unalterable. I *will* be having cookies at the Book Drop meeting tomorrow."

"Oh! Speaking of the Book Drop, we're going to have a new possible member join us tomorrow."

"Really? That's exciting. We certainly have grown since our first meeting, haven't we?"

They had. Their first meeting had been attended by only ten people, and now, they had at least twenty every week and sometimes more.

"Who is it?" Esther asked as they lined up in the shorter self-checkout line.

"My best friend since grade three. She's just moving back to the area."

"Is she a Christian?"

Ava nodded. "That's her. Down there by aisle five with the brown hair and the red jacket."

"She's pretty."

"She is, and she's just as kind as she is pretty."

Esther moved forward to the next available scanner. "See you and your friend tomorrow."

Ava returned her wave as she also moved to a checkout that had just come open. Her phone dinged.

Is it eight yet? Eddie's message read.

Unfortunately, no, she replied.

I wish it was.

Me, too. Still at the library?

Yep.

I'm at Friendly's. She started scanning items and putting them in her bag since the cashier at the podium was staring at her.

Still?

Just checking out and getting glared at for texting. TTYL <3 She stuffed her phone into her pocket and ignored the ding of Eddie's reply. She'd take a few minutes to read it and reread all his other messages in the car while the windows defrosted. She passed the last two items across the scanner and opened her wallet to get her loyalty points card out. With any luck, the ingredients in her bag would turn into something just as sweet as the guy who was so anxious to talk to her that he was wishing time away.

Chapter 15

"Hey."

Eddie jumped at Trish's greeting.

"Caught you smiling again," she teased. "Thinking about Ava?"

Eddie's ears began to feel warm. "Yes." He had been doing little else for nearly twenty-four hours now. Ever since Ava had kissed his cheek just over there. He glanced toward the glass doors that led to the entryway.

"I'm glad." Trish pulled out a chair and sat down next to the second computer at the front desk, placing the armload of books she held in her lap. "You know it wasn't that long ago that I suggested you should date her."

"Nope. It wasn't. I guess you were right."

"What was Trish right about?" Lacey asked as she came to join them. "I need the new magazines that Jenna said were behind the desk."

Eddie rose from his chair to get them from her.

"I was right that Eddie should date Ava."

Lacey laughed. "Even Will knew they should date each other."

Eddie rolled his eyes as he handed the magazines to Lacey. "Fine. Everyone was right except me."

Trish shook her head. "Nah, you knew. You just didn't want to know."

"That makes no sense."

"Sure it does," Lacey said. "We all saw how you watched her. Your heart knew before your head did, that's all."

"Hearts can be wrong, you know. They can trick you. Just ask my dad. He says it often enough in his sermons."

Lacey's eyes narrowed. "And sometimes your heart is right."

"I'm just happy to see you smiling again," Trish inserted.

"What do you mean *again*?" Eddie asked.

"You lost your grin for a bit."

"It was lost in the confusion between head and heart most likely," Lacey arched her left brow and gave him a challenging look.

Eddie simply shook his head. Girls were such silly creatures at times. Heads talking to hearts? He chuckled silently. It was probably logical to those who thought happily ever afters were possible. His head and heart had not been at odds. They had both been interested in Ava nearly from the first time he had met her. It was neither head nor heart that had held him back from taking Trish's advice. The stumbling block had been his ability to accept someone who didn't just read romance – but lived, breathed, and wrote it. Not to mention the fact that he was her editor which had caused him to worry about some ethical line being crossed or a job being lost if things did not go well.

"He's still rather jumpy," Trish was back to teasing. It was no wonder she and Henry got along so well. Henry could be quite tormenting when he wanted to be.

"Do you think he's hiding secrets?" she asked Lacey, who smiled as she shook her head.

"That doesn't seem like an Eddie thing. So, I'm going to say no he's not unless you don't know about that kiss he gave Ava yesterday."

"Nope. I know about that."

"How do either one of you know about that?"

"I saw it," Lacey said.

"And I heard Ava telling Gran about it not long ago."

Eddie groaned. Gran knew? Of course, she did. You couldn't keep anything from that woman!

"I suppose if he has a secret, it could be about how he did more texting Ava than data entry yesterday after she left," Lacey suggested.

"I sent her like five texts," Eddie protested, "and how did you know I was texting Ava? I could have been texting anyone."

Lacey pointed to her lips. "It was in your cute little smile while you were doing it. I figured you probably didn't text anyone else while wearing that expression."

Eddie rubbed his face with his hands. "Do either of you know of any librarian positions open at any schools? I didn't see any listed the last time I looked."

Both Lacey and Ava looked at him in surprise. "Why?" they chorused.

"Because none of my relations work in any school." He leveled a displeased glare at both of them, which only caused them to laugh.

"Okay, okay," Lacey said. "I'll leave you alone about Ava for now and go put these magazines where they belong." She tipped her head and studied him. "Are you hiding something?"

"Would I tell you if I was? Not that I am," he added quickly. He was, but he'd rather that both Lacey and Trish not know about that. He glanced at Trish. He didn't think she had figured out yet that he was Ava's new editor.

"Twitchy," Trish said catching his glance. "Jumpy and twitchy – both are good signs of hiding something." She gave him a sneaky smile. "Both Lacey and I know all about that."

Lacey chuckled and agreed as his phone dinged.

"Oooh, is it from Ava?" Trish asked.

"Yep." She had sent him an email, apparently. He angled his phone away from where either Trish or Lacey could see it before he started typing.

Is it about what we talked about last night?

During their phone conversation, Ava had mentioned a second pen name to him. This one also wrote romance but not just any sort of romance. It was romance that featured characters from Jane Austen's novels. He had spent a couple of hours last night looking up her other work and scanning some fanfiction forum she had mentioned. Had he known about this part of her writing, would he have come to his decision to date her as soon as he did? He wasn't sure he would have. But that being said, he also knew that eventually he would have found a way around his reasons to not date her. There was just something about her. And no, it wasn't his heart telling his head what to do.

Yep. Manuscript. Let me know if you can tolerate it or if it's just not serious enough to tempt you, she replied.

See what I did there? A second text from her pinged in and was accompanied by a crying, laughing emoji.

I'm Edmund. Not Darcy. He felt his lips twitch up higher on one side that another as he enjoyed his witty rejoinder.

Bahahaha!

His smile grew at her amused response.

"See, there's that smile," Lacey said before heading toward the magazine racks at the back of the library.

"She's right. It's a cute smile," Trish said. "Unfortunately, I'm taken, so I can only admire it as an older sister would." She ignored his withering glare. "So, what are you two hiding?"

He shook his head as the entry doors opened.

"Hello, Trish." A gentleman whom Eddie had never seen before approached the desk.

"Oh, hi, Mr. Johnston. Ava's in the computer room."

Eddie felt his eyes grow wide as his heart began beating faster. This was Ava's dad? She had said he might come looking for him, but he'd hoped it wouldn't be for a while, if ever.

"I'm not here for her." He pulled his gloves off and smiled at Eddie. It was a friendly expression. That was good right?

"Are you Eddie?"

"I am."

The man stuck out his hand. "Dick Johnston. I'm pleased to meet you. I hear you've been reading my little girl's stories and that you don't believe in happily ever afters, and since it seems that you like her enough to allow her to help you cook your food – a potentially dangerous proposition – I thought I should find out what kind of fellow you are."

"You read Ava's stories?" Trish whispered.

Eddie nodded. "I'm her editor, and yes, I do like her enough to want to date her," he added to Mr. Johnston.

"You're her editor?" Trish asked.

"Yes."

"Is that the secret?" Trish whispered.

"Yes." He swallowed as he saw Mr. Johnston's brow furrow. "I asked Ava not to tell anyone I was her editor." It seemed like a good idea to just come clean up front with her father. "I've been rather outspoken about my condemnation of romance as trite, and as you said, I've argued with more than one female of my acquaintance about the fact that happily ever afters are not real because no one can be happy all the time forever." He drew in a deep breath and blew it out quickly.

Ava's father chuckled. "Ah, I see. You're a bit of a literalist about it, are you?" He shook his head. "That won't fly with Ava."

"No, sir, it doesn't."

"But you do believe in marrying until death do you part and treating your wife as though she's the most precious thing to you – because she is?"

Eddie nodded.

"Even when she's disagreeable? Because Ava can argue. It's her second superpower, just behind writing."

"Yes, sir, and I know, sir."

"Good." He put his gloves back on. "Then, I think we should get along quite well. I won't tolerate anyone treating her poorly."

"I wouldn't expect you to."

"Aren't you going to say *hi* to Ava?" Trish asked him.

"Nope. Because if I do, she's going to ask me what I'm doing in Hatfield Falls, and I'm going to have to admit that I'm Christmas shopping, and she already knows that I bought her sister and mother a gift which means I'm shopping for her." He wore a large smile as he spoke. "It's hard to keep things from her. At least, it is for me." He looked at Eddie. "Do you drink coffee?"

"Sometimes. But I prefer tea."

"Tea?" His eyebrows rose high. "Well, they sell that along with coffee at Tim's. I'll have Ava arrange a time for you and her to meet her mother and me for tea." His friendly smile faded as Sam approached the front desk. The fellow had been prowling the book aisles for about half an hour and held a couple books which he placed on the self-checkout scanner.

"Mr. ... Mr. Johnston," Sam stammered when he saw Ava's dad.

"I heard you got sent down." Mr. Johnston stepped close to him. "Perhaps if you had learned to keep your commitments as a young man, you would have lasted longer on the team. What are you doing in Hatfield Falls?"

There was no joviality to the man's tone. In fact, it was calm, cool, and rather frightening. Eddie made a mental note to never give Mr. Johnston a reason to use that tone with him.

"Penance and putting my university degree to use."

"I'll give your appreciation for a career to fall back on to Ava."

"She was an excellent English tutor." He sounded genuine enough.

"Mmm," her father grunted. "She doesn't tutor anymore."

"That's too bad, now isn't it?" Sam had puffed out his chest a bit – much like a gorilla who had been challenged.

"Not really. She found she didn't like it after that last fellow she worked with turned out to be... well, I think you know what he was. Not that she knows I know." He blew out a breath. "History aside, I hope you settle in well to whatever it is that you are now doing."

"Just so long as it has nothing to do with your daughter?" There was a slight sniping taunt to his voice.

"Something like that."

"Yeah, well, it seems she has a boyfriend anyway." He jerked his head in Eddie's direction. "Or at least she did the other day, when he interrupted our reunion."

Mr. Johnston smile returned. "Why, yes, she does have a boyfriend, and he's a fine young man." He clapped Sam on the shoulder. "I won't keep you from what you need to do." He looked at Eddie. "I'll have Ava tell you when we're getting together." He gave a nod and left.

"I need to sign in to the archives," Sam said to Eddie as he finished checking out his books and waited for the receipt to print. "Do we still do that here or has that changed?"

"No, it hasn't changed. I'll just send your details up to Stuart, and he'll buzz you in when you get there." Eddie opened the archive sign in. "Do you have a photo ID that I can scan in?"

"Driver's license work?"

"Sure does." Eddie took his license and placed it on the scanner. This way Stuart would know that the person at the door was the person he was supposed to let in. They only had one librarian in the archives and only on certain days and at certain times. The archives weren't that big, nor were they heavily used. "Doing some research?" he asked to fill the space between him and Sam as he waited for the scanned picture to load on his computer screen.

"Yeah; they have me doing grunt work over at the paper. I guess that's how they weed out the wanna bes from the real reporters, or so they tell me."

"Anything interesting?" Trish asked.

Sam turned a charming smile on her.

"She's engaged to my brother," Eddie inserted before Sam could answer.

The guy shook his head. "You just can't let me flirt with anyone can you?" He laughed. "Nah, nothing interesting yet, and nothing I'm free to share anyway. I'd rather not be the new guy who gave away a lead or something."

"Makes sense I suppose," Trish replied. "You wouldn't want to lose a job before you even really had it."

"Exactly."

"You're all set." Eddie handed Sam's license back to him. "Stuart will record when you leave, so no need to stop here on your way out. The archives close at four thirty today."

Sam blew out a breath. "Small towns and their early hours," he muttered. "Thanks, man. For this." He lifted the license and looked up. "Not for ruining all my fun with the pretty ladies."

"So, that was interesting," Trish said when he had left. "Do you plan to tell every guy who smiles at me to back off?"

Eddie shot her a smile. "Yep. Especially when they have a less than stellar reputation when it comes to treating ladies properly."

"Awww." She gave his shoulder a thump with her fist. "You're so sweet. Ava's a lucky girl, and speaking of Ava..."

Here it came. The secret he had hoped Trish had forgotten about. "I assume you know what she writes."

"Oh, I sure do."

"Please, don't tell anyone that I'm her editor."

"Why?"

"Well, for starters, that would give away her secret of being a romance writer, and then, because I..." How was he supposed to put into words what being exposed for being so vocally wrong about romance meant for him.

"Because you have always said horrible things about romance and people who read them."

"I wouldn't say horrible, but yeah." He blew out a breath. "I've always been the nerdy, book-loving brother who prided himself on being well-educated and right." He shrugged. "I'm not sure who I'd be if that were to go away."

Trish sighed and shook her head. "You'd still be exactly who you are. No one would think less of you."

"But," he looked around and then lowered his voice, "I like her books."

She pressed her lips together and visibly took a moment to compose herself before responding. "Liking romance does not make you less of who you are. So what if you were wrong about something?" She placed the book she held in her hand on top of the pile on the table next to her and stood up. "You're still Eddie."

She came to lean against the desk next to him and poked his chest. "In here, you're still the same. Your identity is not what you do or what others say you are. Trust me. I know. Your identity is who you are. It's how God created you to be, and it seems that he created you to be someone who loves an author and her books. I think that's awesome, and don't worry, I'll only tell Henry about this because we promised that we wouldn't have any secrets and he already knows what Ava writes."

Eddie closed his eyes. "But Henry? Really?" Of all his brothers to find out his secret, why did it have to be the one most prone to teasing?

"Sorry. I'll tell him not to tease you, but I can't promise he won't. I can't even promise that I won't." She winked at him and then went to get the books from the table so that they could get put in the send out to other libraries box.

Eddie took out his phone. *Trish knows I'm your editor. Your dad was here. He saw Sam. We're going to have tea with your mom and dad sometime. Also, I think he might like me – your dad, not Sam. Hahaha. I'm off in an hour. Want to grab something to eat at the diner?*

What? My dad was here? He likes you?

Yes

Where's Sam?

Archives. You're safe, or I'd be there with you now.

heart-eyes emoji Sorry, I can't do the diner. I'm going out with Nikki before going to the Book Drop meeting.

Oh, right. I forgot. She had told him that last night.

I'll call you after, and I'm coming up to the front now if you're going to still be there in five minutes. I need to know what my dad said.

I'll be here. He looked at those three words and expelled a breath as the truth of them hit him full force and he knew he'd do his best to always be here for her. Okay, so maybe his heart was a step ahead of his head. Not that he was going to share that realization with either Trish or Lacey.

Chapter 16

LATER THAT DAY, AFTER a good conversation with Eddie and sweet kiss to her cheek, Ava slipped into the booth across from Nikki at the Falls Diner. "How was your day? Have you seen any good property listings?"

"I haven't even looked. I suppose I should, but I've barely opened my suitcase as it is. And my container of stuff won't arrive until December seventh. Dad said it can sit in the driveway for as long as I need it to, which means my motivation to find housing is reliant solely upon how long I can tolerate paying for the container rental and how long it takes until being a fully-grown woman living with her parents drives me nuts." Nikki opened her menu. "Wow, things haven't changed much since high school, have they?"

Ava chuckled. "Nope. Same old diner goodness – just new prices to keep up with the times."

"Remember when we came here just after I got my driver's license and celebrated with chocolate milkshakes and french fries?"

"I do. That was our first foray into independence."

And once they had gotten a taste of it, they had craved more and more. Neither she nor Nikki were the sort of person to live at home any longer than necessary. They had both sought their own lives as soon as graduation was over – well, Nikki had perhaps been more adventurous, since she had gone off to university and then out to Edmonton.

Ava had skipped university in favour of starting her writing career. She had also, when compared to Nikki, always been more of the type to stick close to home. She liked the familiar. It was cozy. Comfortable. Where she belonged.

"I am not getting a milkshake tonight," Nikki said with a laugh. "And not just because it's cold out. I haven't signed up for a gym to work it off at yet, and we know I'm having french fries – since I can't resist them – and one of the classic dinner burgers – because, well, burger, yum – so working it off would have to happen."

"So are you saying that a bacon cheeseburger and fries are fine but a milkshake along with it would push it over the top?" It sounded about right for how Nikki rationalized things – indulgence was necessary, but with "moderation."

"Yep, that's Nikki logic."

Indeed, it was. "Nikki logic might want to work delicious baked goods into her what to eat to not have to work out equation because the treats at our Book Drop meeting are not to be missed."

Nikki peeked over the top of her menu at Ava. "You didn't mention baked goods yesterday. They're good, huh?"

"I'm having the chicken breast and a side of veggies if that answers your question, and I'm drinking water but getting a large hot chocolate to go."

Nikki sighed. "Do you know if any gyms in Wilson's Crossing or Hatfield Falls have day passes?"

"I can Google it if you want." You wouldn't know it to look at her, but there was not much that Nikki liked better than a bacon cheeseburger and fries.

Nikki waved the suggestion away. "It's the holidays... next month. I might as well get a start on my holiday eating plan now. I'll just take a couple of walks with Mom. You know she's into long distance walking now, don't you?"

"No, I hadn't heard."

"She started it just last month. I have no idea why she would start something like that with winter right around the corner, but you know my mom."

"Today is the best day to do what you want to get done," Ava quoted.

"Exactly, so today is the best day for me to eat the food that I want to eat, and tomorrow can be the best day to take a walk. She even has some ladies from church going with her. I'm surprised you hadn't heard about it there."

"I'm going to church in Hatfield Falls with Ali and Riley now."

Nikki's eyes grew wide. "You are? Which church?"

"Hatfield Falls Christian – the one Eddie's dad is pastor of."

"Ah, so now we get to the real incentive – Library Guy."

"Well, not really, but I have to admit the fact that he and his family are there does make the switch easier. You'll meet his grandmother, his sister-in-law Lacey, and his soon-to-be sister-in-law Trish tonight. You might even get to meet his mom if she comes and his sister Emma if she's there. She usually is. It's just Mrs. Bennett who is less frequently there. Sometimes she has other pastor's wifey things to do with her husband, but she tries to make it to a meeting every couple of months. You'll like them."

"I think I have to if I want to keep on the friends list." Nikki bit the end of her straw and smiled. "I'm happy to see you so animated about so many people. At the end of high school and even when I was in uni, you were kind of a loner. I mean, I get why – you had taken one too many hits, as it were. It's nice to see you moving past that."

"They make it easy, and I think I've been past that stuff for a while. Well, maybe not past Mrs. Norris, but the rest. Things change once the diplomas are handed out and all the mean guys and girls have moved away or are too busy facing real life to even remember you."

"True. Is Mrs. Norris still giving you a hard time about the books you read?"

"No, but she does still ask me if I'm 'walking with the Lord' every time I see her, and you know she means have I given up those romance books." Mrs. Norris could try the patience of an angel with her very particular list of *do*s and *don't*s that she was convinced everyone needed to follow or they were in danger of hellfire. Reading romance books was on her list of *don'ts*. "She'd be shocked to know that there is a group of about twenty, mainly Christian..." She raised her eyebrows over a pointed look to emphasize just how shocked Mrs. Norris would be about that fact. "...Ladies, who meet once a month to discuss romances."

"I'm sure she'd start a prayer chain for them." Nikki barely refrained from laughing as she shook her head. "She's one of a kind, thankfully. Pastor does try to keep her in check as much as he can."

The fact that she was the pastor's mother-in-law did make that a bit of a challenge for the man, but Ava had to agree, Pastor Hill did attempt to keep her from doing too much damage. Still, Ava was not about to tell the woman that she not only still read romance, but she also wrote it. There was no telling what kind of lecture and intervention measures would be undertaken by Mrs. Norris before her son-in-law could stop her.

"Hi, Ava. What can I get you?" Pam Lally snapped her gum as she poised her pen over her order pad.

"Chicken and veggies." Ava pointed to the item on the menu. "Water to drink and a big cup of hot chocolate to go when we're done with our dinner. Make that two hot chocolates."

"I could get my own," Nikki grumbled. "But thank you."

"Pam, this is my friend Nikki. You probably saw us in here back in our high school days, but I wouldn't expect you to remember. We weren't regulars."

"You're from around here?" Pam asked Nikki.

"Wilson's Crossing. I was out in Edmonton for a while, but I'm back."

"Well, welcome home, my dear. It's a great place to call home, you know."

"Indeed, I do."

"And what would you like to eat tonight?"

"The classic bacon cheeseburger with fries and water to drink, since I'm saving calories for baked goods later."

Pam chuckled. "Sounds like a good thing to save them for. Where are you two off to after this that has baked goods?"

"A book club meeting."

Pam's lips tipped up into a smile that was higher on one side than the other. "Now that sounds like fun. I enjoy reading, too."

"Oh, well," Ava dug around in her purse and pulled out a folded piece of paper. "This is the book club. We call it the Book Drop, and we meet the third Thursday night each month at Gran's apartment building – I mean Mrs. Green's apartment building."

"Gran attends?"

Ava nodded. "I don't know if you get evenings off or not, but we'd love to have you."

"What book are you reading right now?"

"Oh, we don't have an assigned book."

"You don't? That's different."

"It is different. We just meet to discuss what we've been reading and share recommendations. And eat cake, cookies, and squares. It's bring your own beverage, which is why we need the hot chocolates to go. Nikki is going to the meeting with me." Was there anything that gave her a bigger jolt of excitement than talking about reading books and eating sweets? Probably talking about writing or... well... Eddie.

"I tell you what. I'll put in this order and then take a minute to request to join the social media group to get announcements, and maybe I'll join you some time. I'd like to. I really would. I might even have to request that day off from Dad."

Pam's dad, Paul, owned the diner. Eventually, the place would become Pam's if she wanted it. At least, that's what Eddie had told Ava. She took out her phone. "I'll be waiting to approve your request."

"You really like books, huh?" Pam asked with a chuckle.

"You have no idea," Nikki answered. "She's a true bibliophile, and she needs to give me a link to join said group," she added with a pointed look for Ava as Pam moved on to another booth between where they were sitting and the kitchen. The diner was filling up fast.

"Sorry. I forgot about that last night. I was just so surprised to see you." She found the link and texted it to Nikki. "There."

"What's the most interesting book that has been shared recently?" Nikki asked as she put in her request to join.

"There was a book by A.J. Norland last month that someone introduced the rest of the group to, and they've also been reading some Avery-Anne Johns's books."

Nikki flopped against the back of the seat. "They read your books – like all of them, both pen names?"

"Shhhhh. That's still a secret."

"You mean they don't know?"

"Not many do know except you, Trish, Eddie – because he's my editor – his grandmother – because she's Gran – and my family."

"That makes it a bit awkward at book club, doesn't it? Why don't you tell them? I bet they'd be thrilled to know you were an author, unless they don't like your books?"

"No, so far, they've enjoyed them all, but..." She blew out a breath. "You know what happened when Jenny Kay found my writing notebook back in grade eleven." She shook her head. That hadn't been a fun experience – in fact, the nickname it gave her had followed her through the rest of her high school days. "I'd just rather that no one knew who I was as an author."

"Ava." Nikki reached across the table and took her hands. "We're adults. I'm pretty sure no one is going to publish excerpts from your books in the paper and start calling you Ava the Forlorn."

"Thank you for bringing that name up." She tried to pull her hands away from Nikki, but the woman had some serious grip strength.

"You don't still use the names of guys you have crushes on in your stories, do you?"

Ava shook her head. "I only needed to have that sort of secret discovered and published to the whole school once to learn my lesson about it. However, I have used some of those lovely people who taught me that lesson as inspiration for evil characters. I've even killed off one or two of them."

Nikki shook her head. "Then, I don't know why you won't share your wonderful talented self with the world. Your readers would love you as much as I do. I know they would. And you know, there was something good that came from the humiliating press you got in high school – you earned some good money tutoring that summer and the following year."

Finally, her friend released her hands and Ava tucked them under the table. "It also led to the whole Sam stood me up for being a prude and made sure everyone knew it fiasco." And that was when she had decided that real life was too much for her to deal with and had sealed herself away in her writing world for a couple of years to let the wounds scab over and begin to heal into unsightly, but less painful, scars. "I don't fit when people know who I really am."

"You fit with me, and it sounds like you fit with Trish and Gran and Eddie."

She hated it when Nikki used her non-crazy Nikki logic on her. "I'd just rather not tell anyone. I'm safe just as I am."

"But you're not being your true self."

"Yes, I am. I tell people I write. Freelance. I just don't tell them what it is that I write."

"You're hiding yourself."

She absolutely was – purposefully. "And it's a wise choice. This way, I don't have to deal with the Jenny Kays of this world or Mrs. Norris staging an intervention for my wayward soul."

"And you're limiting how God could use you."

"I don't see how."

"Well, neither do I, but I do know that my mom once told me that I had to be me – completely, authentically me – because that's how God made me and how He planned to use me." Nikki held up her hands and made a face that said she didn't understand it completely either. "I know, but Mom's as wise as she is nutty."

That was true. And Ava knew that her mom's advice was why Nikki was now an engineer rather than being what Nikki had thought was more acceptable for her to be as girl – a science or math teacher.

But tell everyone that she wrote romance? Ava shuddered inwardly. No way. A few trusted friends were enough. The rest of the world could just continue on as they were, enjoying her books and wondering who she really was.

Chapter 17

"So, how'd teatime with the 'rents go today?" Blake asked as he shoved his way into a spot between his brother Tyler and the end of the couch in front of the tv at Henry's house the following Sunday evening. It was comfortably a three-person piece of furniture. Blake, it seemed, was convinced as always that it could hold four adults, which meant Eddie was now snuggled up tightly with the other end of the couch on one side and Fred on the other. He'd wait a few minutes and then find a reason to extract himself to sit somewhere more comfortable. There was no way he was going to watch a full football game like this.

"It was good." At least, he thought it had been good, and Ava had seemed pleased with how things went as well.

"But your lady's not here."

"And that's a problem, why?" Lacey's sister, Cari was seated in a bean bag chair next to Blake's feet. She and Blake had yet to figure out a way to be in the same room without arguing.

"Because it indicates that things might not have gone well. Duh."

"Or," Cari countered, "perhaps it just means she doesn't like football."

"Do you like football?"

Cari shrugged. "I'm here for the snacks."

"Does Ava like snacks?" Blake leaned forward to look down the couch to Eddie.

"As far as I know."

Blake turned back to Cari. "So, she likes snacks, and she's not here. That equals potential troubles for the kid bro."

Eddie sighed. He had always been, and likely would always be, "the kid bro" to Blake. Once Blake gave you a name that he liked, it just sort of hung around whether you liked it or not. "There's no real or potential trouble. Okay?"

"I'm glad to hear it." Blake bit into a slice of pizza. "So are you the next Bennett to get married?" he asked while he chewed.

Eddie shook his head. "I really couldn't tell you. I'm not sure what Fred or Brandon have planned."

Henry chuckled. "Good answer, but it didn't sound like you're planning to avoid marriage."

"I've never planned to avoid it." He could feel his ears growing warm. He had actually been thinking about it more in the past month than he ever had before in his life – except for when he had been given that one life lessons math assignment back in grade nine that forced him to create an imaginary future, complete with a household budget. "Remember, I'm Mom's favourite."

"You are not. I am," Fred teased.

"More like Will is," Brandon said.

"Nope. Eddie's right," Will chimed in. "He's always been Mom's favourite... son," he added when Emma shouted "Hey!" from the kitchen.

"When isn't Eddie right?" Henry said with a laugh.

"Well, he has questionable taste in literature." Emma had rejoined the group in the living room.

"No way! There will to be no debates over romance novels during a football game," Blake said.

"Well, I plan to read a romance novel during the game." Emma shot Eddie a taunting look. "See." She held up her book, and Fred jabbed him in the ribs with his elbow.

"Looks good." He knew it was good. He had read that and all of Ava's other books, except for the ones he had just discovered she had under a different pen name.

"That's all you're going to say?" Emma asked.

Eddie shrugged. "Hope it doesn't get too loud for you?"

His sister's brow furrowed. "Thanks? I think. If it does, Cari and I'll just go downstairs to the family room."

"Not without snacks," Cari muttered.

"Oh, never without snacks." Emma chuckled.

"I'll come with you if you go. I'm okay with just hearing the final score and seeing highlights later," Esther said and then continued her conversation with Emma while completely ignoring Blake's grumble about girls not appreciating football. "Have you started that book yet?"

Emma nodded. "It's really good. I'm glad Gran recommended it."

"Oh, I completely agree. I've actually read the whole series – one right after the other. I was just too interested in what happened to everyone to stop."

"What is it with girls and romance?" Tyler asked with a laugh.

"No debates about romance," Blake repeated. "We're here for the Grey Cup not frou-frou books."

"Frou-frou? Really?" Cari huffed in disdain.

"Yes, really."

"No arguments at all," Lacey said. "If you two can't be civil, one of you might need to watch the game alone. Or sit with me while I read a frou-frou book."

Eddie chuckled. Lacey was a bit of a mother hen and hated, absolutely hated, arguments, which was the exact opposite of her sister Cari, who seemed to thrive on a bit of debate.

"Are you all reading romances?" Blake sounded utterly baffled by the thought.

"Nope," Trish inserted. "I'm reading a women's fiction novel right now."

Blake leaned forward and looked at Eddie. "Kid bro, what's the difference between a romance and women's fiction?"

"Romance has a love story as the central plot and is required to end in a happily ever after or a happy for now. Women's fiction books center on the journey a woman takes through the story. They may or may not have romantic elements, and they can have any sort of ending they want."

"Ah, so less frou-frou." Blake nodded his head as if he understood.

Again, Cari huffed.

"Blake finds all books to be a bit frou-frou," Tyler said. "At least all the fiction ones."

Eddie shook his head and chuckled. He was just wondering how an author such as Frank Peretti or Ted Dekker would react to hearing their books being labelled as *frou-frou* when his phone buzzed, drawing his attention to it.

Ava? That was unexpected. She had said she'd talk to him after the game. "Hey, what's up?" he asked as he stood and started to leave the room.

"Is that Ava?" Blake asked.

"Yeah," Freddie answered. "Saw the name," he added when Eddie turned to scowl at him.

"You know my pen names are secret, right?" Her voice didn't sound right. Something was wrong. He hurried from the room and started down the stairs.

"Yeah, I do."

She sniffled. Yep, something was definitely wrong. "Then why did you tell Sam that I'm Avery-Anne?"

Eddie took the final four steps to the basement in one jump. "What are you talking about?" He jogged down the short hall to his room. This conversation was not one that anyone needed to overhear.

"My dad just got a call from Mrs. Norris to express her concern about the kinds of things I write." Another sniffle.

"Who's Mrs. Norris?"

"An old lady at our church who thinks romances are Satan's entertainment for young ladies." A large exhale. "She told my dad I was writing porn." The admission came out in a whisper.

"Porn? That's ridiculous." How was anything Ava wrote even close to porn? There was nothing more physical than a kiss or two in her books.

"I know it is, but..." The phone went silent except for a couple of sniffles.

"Ava, why do you think I told Sam that you're Avery-Anne?" He could hear her crying now. Softly, but it was unmistakable.

"There's a story in the entertainment section of the paper. It's not big, but it's there. Oh, this is going to be just like high school all over again."

He had never heard her so panicked. It was very unlike the Ava he knew. His Ava was confident and sure of herself. This Ava was the furthest thing from that. This Ava was the one he had seen briefly on the other side of the chink in her armor at their last movie night. Whatever had happened in Ava's past must have been horrible to turn a confident person like her into the anxiety filled one on the other end of this conversation. His heart hurt for her while at the same time he felt offended that she would accuse him of telling her secret.

"I don't know what happened in high school, Ava, but I doubt anything that happened there would repeat itself in the real world. High school is not reality. It's just a weird space, and I still don't know why you think I told Sam about your pen name."

She blew out a breath. "I looked it up online – the article that Mrs. Norris told Dad about – and it says that Sam discovered that his former English tutor from high school was now a published author."

"Ok, but I'm still not seeing how that means I told him."

"He got that information from a source at the library."

"It still doesn't mean it was me."

"Who else knows?" Her tone was full of sniffles and exasperation.

"Gran and Trish both know."

"But they wouldn't tell anyone." Her words punched him in the gut.

"And I would?"

"Maybe."

He looked at his phone in disbelief over what he had just heard for a moment before putting it back up to his ear. "You really trust me that much, huh?" The offense he felt was quickly growing. How could she think he would tell anyone that she wrote under either of her pen names?

"Yes – no – I don't know. All I know is that Sam has told the world that I write romance and now Mrs. Norris is going to tell everyone to pray for me because of my great sin, and people are going to stare at me and whisper behind my back."

"You don't know that, and apparently, you don't know me either." And that was what hurt the most. "I thought you did. I thought you were one of the few who knew what kind of nerd I was and didn't care. I thought you knew that I would never want to hurt you or anyone else." He should have never dated a romance writer. They believed in fairytales. Real life was messy and far less fanciful.

"I was wrong," he continued. "I was horribly, horribly wrong." Had he ever been more wrong? Not likely. "I guess the good news is that we found out now that we won't work as a couple. Of course, it would have been better before we started dating." And before he had fallen in love with her. He blew out a soft breath and willed his tears to stay where they were – inside his head.

"I didn't tell Sam anything. I don't know how he found out, but if your first response is to blame me, then, I think it's best if we part ways outside of work, and if you'd rather find a new editor, then, we can break off that relationship, too. Just let me know. I don't have to work at the library until Wednesday this week. So, you won't have to see me on Tuesday. Goodbye, Ava." His composure was fading.

Fast. Anger was filling all the spaces not occupied with pain.

"Wait."

"Why?" In his mind, there was nothing left to talk about.

"If you didn't tell him, then, who did?"

"How would I know?" he snapped. "Perhaps you should call Gran and Trish and accuse them. Maybe they know." He punched the end call button with his finger. It wasn't nice. He knew it wasn't. However, he really didn't care at the moment. How dare she assume he would share her secret! He paced small circles around his room while he attempted to gain control of his anger and hurt.

So much for watching the game. He sat down at his desk and drummed his fingers on it while staring at the ceiling. There was no way he was going to be able to be anything but an utter grouch if he went upstairs. How could he be anything else when the woman he loved thought he was no better than the guy she had written and killed off as the villain in one of her books?

He picked up his phone. *See. Happily ever afters aren't real*, he typed. Deleted. Retyped. Re-deleted. It was true. And yet, with all his heart he wished it wasn't.

He scrubbed his face with his hands. What had happened to her in high school? It had to be more than just being stood up by Sam.

He opened his laptop. He might as well read whatever had started this. He waited while the computer logged him on to the internet. Then, he navigated to the newspaper's website. He should be able to read a couple of issues before they started to lock him out until he bought a subscription. He clicked on entertainment and scrolled past an article about some movie that was delayed, and found an article entitled "The Secrets We Keep."

Eddie read quickly, skimming over the opening about dreams of being drafted to the NHL and failure. There, in the middle of a paragraph about needing to improve his grade in English to land a scholarship, was one line. One sentence. The sentence.

Imagine my surprise to arrive back in my high school stomping ground to discover, via a source at the library, that the girl who helped me land that scholarship and sparked my interest in writing, Ava Johnston, or Avery-Anne Johns as she is known to her readers, had become what appears to be quite a successful romance author.

He went on for a bit about how he had learned quite a bit from Ava and had actually found journalism to be a good fit as a major in university. Then, he said:

Before I close in a fashion that will satisfy both my editor and my former tutor, I want to encourage my readers to check out Avery-Anne's books at the Hatfield Falls library, where I know they have several on their shelves, minus the two which are sitting on my nightstand as I write this. One is half-read, and so far, the story reminds me of the girl I knew back when I was a just a teenage jerk who was full of more testosterone than good sense.

The story is sweet and funny, with a touch of sass and characters who act on both convictions and the occasional ill-thought-out impulse. In other words, it's a delight, and yes, folks, you're reading this right. I, a hockey-loving goal-chaser turned seeker of a newsworthy story, apparently now read romance. I'm not sure if my foray into this genre of fiction will stick, but I'm quite content to enjoy this land of Avery-Anne-created happily ever afters while I'm here.

This was followed by an acceptable conclusion that tied the article into a neat little bow and reminded readers of what he had said at its outset. All-in-all it was a well-written piece. The fellow had learned how to craft an interesting tale, and in the process of skimming and reading, Eddie's anger from just minutes ago was beginning to dim. Perhaps he could rejoin the party upstairs and enjoy some of the game.

He copied the article and pasted it into a Google Doc. Aside from the mention of her name and her pen name, the article was quite lovely and held the potential to help Ava gain fans.

With that done he stood, and then chuckled to himself as he wondered if the second book Sam was about to read was the one with the character based on him that dies before the story finishes.

If only real life were as easy to fix as a story's plot. He stood looking up the stairs. If this were a story he was editing... Hmmm. What suggestions would he give to an author to fix it?

"Hey, kid bro, you okay?" Blake held a plate of food and stood at the top of the stairs. "I was going to bring you snacks."

"You were?" That was odd.

"Yeah, well, Fred was going to, but then Esther asked him about some music thing, so I volunteered."

That made more sense. Fred was easily distracted by all things music. "Is the music for church?"

"No, it's for the holiday concert at her school."

That was interesting.

"You don't look completely okay."

Eddie blew out a breath as he joined Blake at the top of the stairs. "I'm not. It seems there was some trouble I didn't know about."

"With your lady?"

He nodded. "But I'm working on if it can be fixed." He had read enough of her books. Perhaps he could figure out a way to write a happy ending to this newspaper fiasco for Ava. And maybe, if he could convince her that he wasn't what she obviously thought he was, that ending might include him.

Chapter 18

PAIN TORE THROUGH AVA'S heart as her phone went silent. Panic, deep and all-consuming, grasped her. What had she done? She tossed her phone on her bed and flapped her hands in a fan-like fashion in front of her face as she took slow and deliberate breaths. And yet, the pain would not stop. The panic did not lessen. Instead, they twisted her stomach and made her feel faint. Oh, what had she done?

Her tears from earlier started again. Only this time, they weren't because of what someone else had done to her. This was her own doing.

"But if he didn't tell Sam, who did?" she asked Charlie. The little fluff ball yipped in reply but was of no real help. Or maybe, Charlie knew as much as she or anyone else did about who had revealed her secret. She flung herself across the bed in a satisfyingly Marianne Dashwood way before rolling to her side to grab the box of tissues on the nightstand. "Why am I so stupid?"

Again, her question was met with a yip before Charlie joined her on the bed and began licking at her tears.

"Stop that." She pushed her sister's dog away from her face, but it was of no use. If she was going to lie here and cry, Charlie was going to tend to her tears despite being pushed away and scolded. So, Ava sat up to save her face from a canine washing and found her lap immediately filled with a concerned pup.

"You certainly are persistent, aren't you?" She snuggled the dog to her chest to keep its little tongue away from her face.

Her phone buzzed and her heart leapt with hope which flickered and then died when she saw that it was her father and not Eddie who was calling.

"Your mom and I are upstairs, and your mother won't let me come down to your room without making sure it's okay first," her dad said before she could even say hi.

Ava rubbed her face with a tissue to dry her tears. "I'll come upstairs." She sniffed.

"Oh, Ava." Her father's voice was filled with worry. "You're crying, aren't you?"

"Yes, but I'm trying not to, so please don't mention that I am."

"I'm not afraid of your tears."

She chuckled. That was so not true. Tears from any of his ladies – Mom, Ali, Riley, her – were both her father's kryptonite and his source of fuel to see justice served. "Yes, you are, Dad. I'll be right up."

She blew out a breath, took a minute to splash some water on her face at the sink in her ensuite bathroom, and after blowing her nose, climbed the stairs to face her family. They would not be happy to hear that she had overreacted and broken her own heart.

She had only managed to get the door to the basement closed behind Charlie before Riley was attached to her leg and her father had her wrapped in a tight hug. It was enough to overwhelm her resolve not to cry.

"Aba ky. Aba ky." Riley squeezed her leg tighter.

"Yes, Ava is crying," Ali said as she removed Riley from her sister's leg. "Let's get her something for her nose, okay?"

"Shoo shoo. Aba shoo shoo," Riley babbled to Ali, while Ava's father led her to the couch to sit between him and her mother.

"I'll be fine. I just need time to..." She pressed her lips together. To do what? There wasn't anything she could do – it wasn't like she could just take back her accusation or retract that article in the paper. Words once spoken or published could not be erased from all memory as easily as backspacing on a computer keyboard.

"Your father has spoken to Pastor Hill," her mother said, "and Pastor has promised to speak with his mother-in-law."

"But the damage is done," Ava protested.

Her mother took her hand. "If by damage you mean your secret, about using the gift God has given you to brighten the lives of others and place examples of His love in their hands, being shared, then, yes, the damage has been done."

Leave it to her mother to be all that is not soft and cuddly when faced with a problem. It was how she always was when her girls were upset over something. She acknowledged there was an issue, but she always stated it in as truth-forward and encouraging a fashion as she could.

"And for that, I must apologize," her mother continued.

Ava's brow furrowed. "Apologize? I don't understand."

"Your mother and I had a somewhat protracted discussion before deciding to come over to see you. During that discussion we concluded that we were wrong to encourage you to hide what you write. I'll admit that we, too, were afraid of what people like Mrs. Norris would say, but why should we fear her or seek human approval? Do you remember what you told us when you presented us with your decision to not go to university?"

Ava nodded slowly. "I think I told you that God had called me to write." She had felt the truth of that statement with all her heart when she had said it. She still felt that way. It was God who had created her with a love for stories. It was also God who had given her the ability to create the stories she loved.

"You shouldn't hide who God made you to be. Your candle should be set on a hill and not under the basket that your father and I helped provide for you."

"But it's just writing love stories with happy endings." Ava shook her head. "It's not a candle. I mean, it's not like I'm sailing away to a foreign land to start a mission or something."

"Oh, well, I should hope you're not! Can you imagine what Mrs. Norris would have to say about a single lady doing what a 'man ought to do'?" Her mother laughed and so did Ava. She had a point. Mrs. Norris had many loud opinions that she was all-too-willing to share.

"Your calling by God is not less than someone else's," Ali inserted as she placed a box of tissues on her sister's lap. "I'm called to be a single mom and someone's administrative assistant – or so I hope – if one of my resumes does its job. And because I am called to do those things, I must do them as a service to the Lord, knowing that in the process, He can and will use me to fill the earth with goodness and to touch the lives of others. Starting with this one." She gave Riley's cheek a kiss.

"You're also filling the earth with God's goodness, Ava, and in so doing, He has led you to make some wonderful new friends, including a lovely young man who seems to adore you almost as much as I do." Her father smiled as tears once again filled Ava's eyes.

"I may have ruined that," she whispered.

"Oh, no," her mother groaned. "What did you do?"

Ava blew out a breath. "I called Eddie and asked him why he told Sam about my pen name."

This was met with a chorus of her name said quite emphatically.

"I know. It was stupid."

"Excessively," her mother muttered.

"I agree," she said with a shrug. "He broke up with me." The tears that had been hanging onto the rims of her eyes spilled out. She pressed one hand against her stomach to stifle the sobs that wished to overcome her.

"Oh, Ava." Her dad pulled her close to his side with one arm. "I'm sorry that you got hurt, but I can't blame him for doing what he did."

Ava couldn't blame Eddie either, and she wanted to tell her dad that, but at the moment, speaking wasn't possible.

Her dad sighed and rubbed her shoulder. "If it's meant to be, it'll work out," he whispered.

Oh, how she hoped he was right, because if it didn't, she wasn't sure how her heart would ever put itself back together.

On Tuesday morning, Ava was still feeling quite unin-
spired to write warm and fuzzy stories for her characters,
but she knew that her bills would not pay themselves and
that meant she needed to keep writing.

With a looming phone bill as her motivation, she settled
into a study carrel at the Wilson's Crossing library. Here,
there was no Gran across from her to chat with. There was
no Lacey or Trish to greet her. There was no Josh to wave
at her from across the library. And most importantly, there
was no possibility of having to see Eddie.

He had told her that he wasn't going to be at the Hatfield Falls library today, but that didn't matter. Her days
of working in that library were over – except for when Ali
needed her to take Riley to story time. Her heart simply
could not bear to see him unless forced to do so.

She opened her laptop, took out her ideas notebook,
and flipped through the pages without looking at them.
Perhaps she should start with a life update on her blog
– just admit the sad state of her life, confess her utter
foolishness to her readers and move on. If moving on were
possible.

A message from Nikki popped open on her phone
screen. *Where are you?*

Library

*Nope. You're not here. Sadly, neither is your boyfriend
whom I had hoped to meet.*

Oh, no. Nikki didn't know. She hadn't talked to anyone
except Ali in the past two days. *He's not my boyfriend*

anymore. And I'm at the Wilson's Crossings library. Why are you in Hatfield Falls?

Shopping and an appointment with Tiffany – that re-altor your friend Lacey recommended. What do you mean he's not your boyfriend anymore?

Cool. Are you looking at houses today?

If possible, I will. Was hoping you'd go with me. And don't think I didn't notice that you haven't answered my question about Library Guy.

He broke up with me, but he had a good reason so don't blame him.

Shopping will wait. I have just enough time to come pick you up and get back here for my meeting. Pack up.

I can't.

I'm sorry but the number you have texted is unavailable. Your fake-Uber driver will be there to pick you up soon.

Ava huffed. *Pushy much?*

Don't make me come in and make a scene. I hate making scenes.

Fine. Let me write a blog post. I'm in the quiet area near the windows.

As it turned out, Ava was only three-quarters of the way through what was supposed to be an easy post when Nikki arrived. Apparently, publicly admitting your stupidity was harder than sharing wishes and dreams.

"How long until you have to meet with Tiffany?"

Nikki looked at her phone. "Five minutes more than it takes to drive back to Hatfield Falls."

"Well, then, I guess I'll just save this as a draft." It was a relief. Seeing the end of her relationship in black and white was so final. It somehow made it more real.

On the way to Hatfield Falls, Ava told Nikki all about the article in the paper, Mrs. Norris calling her dad who then called Ava, and then, how her anger at Sam bubbled over onto Eddie.

"Not all guys are Sam," Nikki said as she turned off her car. "I know there were others who teased you for telling them that you liked them, but you and I both know it was Sam who destroyed your trust. He was such a good actor." She unbuckled her seatbelt and turned toward Ava. "Stop letting him ruin your whole life instead of just your prom."

"I'm not letting him ruin my life."

Nikki arched one eyebrow. "Your slightly red nose and eyes, as well as that pile of tissue in the trash bin, say otherwise." She held up a hand when Ava opened her mouth to protest. "No, you haven't let him control your whole life. You eventually came out of your cave, but as soon as he reappeared and made you feel..." She waved a hand at Ava in a random pattern. "However it is you were feeling that made you do this to yourself, you gave him control over your life again."

"I would like to lodge a complaint."

"Yes, I know. You dislike it when I say what you don't want to hear."

Ava nodded. "But I think I'm still glad you do."

"That's what friends are for, right?"

Again, Ava nodded.

"Are you ready?" Nikki's hand was on the door handle.

Ava blew her nose one more time and tucked her pack of tissues in her bag. "I could just wait in the car."

"No. It's too cold, and I need you because I hope to find a place that you can share with me – at least for a while. Remember how we used to plan to live together back when we were in high school?"

"I do, but I also remember your mom telling us it wasn't a good idea."

"Yeah, I know she said that, but we're older now. You work at the library a lot. I work in town. We have other things we do on our own. I think we could probably handle it until you finally figure out how to fix this thing with Library Guy and ask him to marry you." She giggled. "You know you might if you think he's taking too long."

Ava couldn't help but laugh. "I would not." Although she really might. It had been her who had first proposed the idea of her and Eddie being more than friends. "Do you really think this can be fixed?"

Nikki shrugged. "Maybe. I mean you did kind of throw him under a bus without proof, so it probably won't be easy, but maybe it can be done. Happy endings aren't just for books, are they? Please, tell me they aren't, because I've yet to find one."

"Book endings are much easier to write than living life is." She followed Nikki's lead and opened her door. "Happily ever afters are real." She said it more to herself than her friend. "Right?"

"Oh, girl, no. Do not tell me you're questioning that! I've always counted on you to tell me that my happily ever after was somewhere out there."

"But what if my happily ever after is like Miss Bates's?"

"You mean, sitting around talking too much and too fast and doting on your niece and living with your mother?"

Ava shuddered. "Not that last part. That is not in my version of this single girl's happily ever after."

Nikki shook her head as they crossed the parking lot. "I seriously doubt that God is going to let you be single. I don't think you're cut out for it."

"But He might. I mean, I need to realize that my future might not look how I've always wanted it to look."

"You've got me there. I can't argue against that since I know we all need to come to terms with that sort of thing, but don't just give up hope. Okay?" She looked up at the sign over their heads. "Here we are."

The door to the realty office opened.

"Ava?"

She swallowed. "Eddie. Hi."

His eyes darted away from her and hers found the salt on the sidewalk far easier to look at than the guy in front of her.

"Just got the keys to the new place." Fred's excited declaration broke the silence that had enveloped Ava. He dangled a set of keys from his finger. "And we're on our way to get an extra set made for my brother and Nate so they can start work." He looked at Nikki and stuck out his hand. "Hi, I'm Fred."

"I'm Nikki, Ava's friend, and this is your brother?"

Fred nodded. "Yep."

"Hi, I'm Eddie."

Nikki shook hands with him.

"I've wanted to meet you, but I wasn't sure I was going to get to."

"Seriously, Nikki?" Ava muttered.

Fred chuckled.

"I've just moved back from Alberta and am planning to start looking for a place to buy," Nikki continued. "Ava's my moral support."

"Because Nikki and her money are not easily parted," Ava quipped and forced a smile to her lips. "We probably shouldn't keep Tiffany waiting." She gave the sleeve of Nikki's coat a little tug.

"Allow me." Eddie opened the door for them and held her gaze for a moment, but she couldn't read his expression. "It was good to meet you, Nikki."

"Maybe I'll see you around?" she replied.

"Maybe."

Nikki pulled Ava close as they entered the office and the door closed behind him. "He's cute."

Oh, Ava knew that. She looked over her shoulder and watched him walking to his car.

"And it didn't seem like he wanted to be your ex."

"But I hurt him." She hadn't trusted him. She had treated him like he was Sam, and he knew it. And over what? Mrs. Norris being... well... Mrs. Norris. Perhaps her mom was right. Perhaps it was time to embrace every aspect of who God had created her to be.

Chapter 19

EDDIE PACED THE SMALL appliances aisle at Drummonds while Fred got two sets of house keys made – one for him, and another for Will and Nate as he had told Ava. He hadn't expected to see her today. And it had hurt just as much or more than he had expected it to. There was a decided lack of spark to her. Her eyes hadn't twinkled. Her lips hadn't twitched in humour. She had looked as if she wished she could hide from the world and not just him.

He picked up a coffee grinder and read the specs to distract himself from thoughts of Ava. Fred would like this one. It was all chrome. Maybe he'd come back and get it, or... He took out his phone and snapped a pic of the box and the shelf label. Maybe he could get Henry to buy it for him and bring it home.

He moved down the aisle and stopped to look at the bread machines.

"Here's your set of keys to my new house." Fred had never sounded so proud of anything. It made Eddie smile to hear it, and smiling was not something he had felt like doing since before Ava's call on Sunday.

"I'm not sure how long you'll need them though." Fred dropped the keys, which were on a keyring with a little metal book hanging on it, into his hand. Of course, Fred would personalize the key ring. It's just how Fred was.

"What do you mean?" Eddie slipped the keys into his jacket pocket.

"I mean, I think you could get back together with Ava." He started walking towards the front of the store.

Eddie followed. "What makes you say that?"

"Well, we discussed the fact that you were going to attempt to fix things, right?"

"Yeah." They had done that on Sunday after the Grey Cup game was over.

"Add that to how earlier Ava couldn't even look at you and had obviously been crying, and I think she'd take you back in a heartbeat."

"She did look like she'd been crying, didn't she?" They hadn't spoken a word about the awkward meeting in front of Tiffany's office on their way to Drummonds. Fred had just ridden in silence as Eddie drove and thought.

"Yep." Fred turned and headed to the automotive department. "Got the keys!" he said when he poked his head into the garage. Even the guy at the appointments desk cheered at the news.

"When's the party?" Someone called from the shop.

"Not until spring. We've got renos to do – and it'll be a respectable party. I don't want the neighbours to hate me." His comments were met with a loud laugh, probably from the guy who was asking about a party.

Fred turned to Eddie as the automatic door opened in front of them. They had parked near the garage, as it often had spots close to the door. "So, what's the plan to fix things?"

Eddie shook his head and shrugged. "I'm not quite sure. I mean I have ideas, but..."

"Just pick one and go with it."

"But what if it's not the best option?"

"Then, have a plan b ready. Seriously, it's not that hard, bro. Mistakes are not the end of the world. I know you disagree, but they're not."

"Not even if the mistake is putting the wrong fluid in the wrong reservoir in an engine?" Eddie opened his car door.

Fred rolled his eyes. "Okay, so maybe some mistakes are the end of an engine, but still the world goes on."

"And if someone hits the detonate button –"

"Okay, okay, okay," Fred interrupted. "There are times when mistakes cause disasters – like if you put salt in a recipe when it should be sugar." He shot Eddie a grin. That had happened when they were little and helping their mom make cookies. "But this is not one of those times. You're going to fix things. It might just take more than one swing of the hammer to ensure that things go back together as they should."

Eddie turned out of Drummonds' parking lot. "I just wish I knew why she was so afraid to have people know her pen names."

"Says the guy who won't tell anyone he's her editor."

"Shut up unless you're going to be helpful."

Fred laughed. "Drop me off at home. I'll take my vehicle out to Will's, and you can go be Encyclopedia Brown."

"Not happening. Prying into her secrets isn't going to make her trust me more."

Fred groaned. "Then, don't pry. Buy her flowers or something."

"I don't see how that's going to help." Ava needed a happily ever after, not a bouquet of roses. "The problem is Sam's unknown source for that article and some old lady named Mrs. Norris." And he wasn't sure how to fix either one of those things unless... He sucked in a quick breath as an idea materialized in his brain. It might just work.

"Figured it out?"

"Maybe. You'll have to drive yourself to Will's." He did have some sleuthing to do.

Five minutes later, as he pulled his car up in front of Henry's house, his phone buzzed. "Gran," he said in reply to Fred's look of curiosity. "Not Ava. You're safe to go do your thing."

"You'll tell me if she calls you, right?"

"Probably."

"Definitely probably?"

"Just get going." There was a link to something that Gran said he needed to see. "Gran says I need to read something." He clicked the link.

"Fine, but I'm your twin so that means I get to know things others don't."

"I know." He waved Fred away as his brow furrowed at the title of the blog Gran had sent him to: *Author in Search of Forever*. Was this Ava's blog? There were pictures of her books in the header. He was just getting set to read the article at the top of the page when another message from Gran popped onto his screen.

This one was a picture. What was she sending him pictures of? He opened the message. It was a screenshot of a social media post.

Are you okay? Is this why Ava wasn't at the library today? I don't know. I think I'm okay or will be.

If you need help... *heart emoji*
Thanks. Love you, too.

First, he enlarged the screenshot. It was a post revealing to her fellow Book Drop members not just her Avery-Anne pen name but also her A.J. Norland one. Apparently, both had been read by Book Drop members. She apologized for not having been open with them about it from the beginning and promised to let them ask her any questions they wanted to at their upcoming Christmas party.

He read the post as second time with a slight smile that couldn't be helped. This took guts, and he was proud of her for her courage. He knew how frightening it was to even contemplate sharing a protected secret. He had felt some of that when he had told Josh that he'd never really had a girlfriend before Ava.

He clicked away from the photo and went back to the blog article.

Dear readers,

As you know, I've written some doozies of messes for my heroes and heroines to overcome in my books. Once again, as I sit here in a gigantic mess of my own creation, I am reminded that while fiction might imitate life, life is not as easy to twist into knots and then, neatly and carefully, untangle them as it is in fiction.

I blew it. I have created my own dark moment. You see, there was an article in the paper on Sunday. In this article, it linked my real name – Ava Johnston – to one of my pen names: Avery-Anne Johns. (A.J. Norland is my other pen name.) Based on what the article said, I assumed that Library Guy was the one who told the reporter.

Library Guy? He guessed that was a better name than Sir Jerk-a-lot.

There's some angsty teenage backstory behind all of this, but suffice it to say, accusing the guy you've fallen in love with of being a snitch is the best way to break your own heart.

She loved him? Again, he found himself smiling because it couldn't be helped. If she loved him, it meant that if he could get things right, he wouldn't have to think about a future without her.

I've told you how wonderful he is.

She had blogged about him? He wasn't sure how he felt about that, though he was glad to know that what she had said was good.

I've even grumbled about his reserved nature that takes a little bit longer to make decisions.

Or at least, partly good.

But have I told you how he's as noble as any Jane Austen hero? Because he is. Now, imagine how one of those characters, such as Mr. Darcy, would respond to being accused of doing something he hadn't done. Picture how he'd be beside himself with indignation at the implication that he was dishonest and untrustworthy. Got the mental image?

The result is heartache.

Library Guy has become my will-never-be-mine prince charming, and it's my fault – not his – that my heart is in a million pieces that keep leaking out of my eyes. I can't blame him for breaking up with me. I'd have broken up with me, too.

That's it for today, guys. I just needed to let you know about my foolishness and to share my real name with you. There are reasons for why I've never shared it before. Some are probably good, though I don't trust my judgment on much of anything at the moment, but none are so good that keeping who I really am a secret becomes so important that the revelation of that secret justifies harming a dear, sweet man.

I'll be back... eventually... likely after all the tissues are gone and it's impossible to shed another tear.

Knowing how greatly her heart was hurting made his own ache more. He had to do something to fix it, if only to see her happy once again. Another idea sparked to life in his mind, and he blew out a breath. It was just the grand gesture that Ava's story needed, but he was going to need some help to pull it off, so a stop at the library would be needed once his detective work was completed.

Two days later, Eddie peeked out the door to the library's back room and to the left. "Is she here?" he asked Josh who was in his usual break spot between the reference books.

"Yep. And she's been looking this direction every few minutes. I'm not sure if she wants to see you or doesn't want to see you. She kinda looks nervous."

"She probably is. I am."

"But she doesn't know what we have planned."

After he had found out what he needed to know at the newspaper office, Eddie had come to the library to talk to Josh and Miranda, his boss. Together, he and Josh had ironed out the details of Eddie's grand gesture, and then, Miranda had given her approval.

"I've got the books for the display on the cart, and Lacey is removing the books from the current display and dusting the shelves while I take my break."

"I've got the sign." Eddie held it up.

Josh's watch beeped. "Sounds like it's time. Was Miranda really okay with this?"

"She's thrilled. She loves highlighting local books and authors. I just hope Ava isn't angry about it." Grand gestures always came with great risk in novels – and real life.

"Well, I think it's cool."

"But you're not a girl."

Josh chuckled. "My sister thought our plan was sweet, if that helps."

"A bit." Eddie squared his shoulders and took out his phone. "And you're really sure this reply to her blog post is good?" He had let Josh read it this morning.

"Yeah. I wish I could write that well. I'd sure have better grades in English if I did – and probably a girlfriend."

"Still haven't gotten Skye to go out with you?"

"Haven't asked yet."

"Don't wait too long."

"I won't." The kid blew out a breath as if even the idea of asking the girl he liked out was overwhelmingly frightening.

Eddie understood that feeling. In fact, it swirled inside him right now as he clicked the reply button on Ava's blog and watched the circle of dots spin before his words appeared on the screen. He had never, in all his life, posted a reply to a blog post he had read, and this reply? His first one? This one was heart-on-his-sleeve personal.

"*Operation Tell the World I Read Romance* has commenced," he said to Josh as he followed him and the book cart to the front bookshelf display that stood across from the information desk.

He typed *posted* into the messaging app on his phone and sent it to Gran. She was going to "happen" to read the reply he had just made and be all shocked about it in such a way that Ava would want to know what was wrong. Eddie almost wished he could be there to see how that went, but he and Josh had a book display to construct before Eddie's "special guest" arrived.

"It's all ready for the new display," Lacey said. "And I now have more books to shelve." She paused when Eddie stood his sign – which was a piece of printer paper held in an acrylic page display holder – on top of the bookshelf.

He looked at his phone when it buzzed. *Oh, Eddie! I haven't finished reading your post, but I know I'm not going to have to act at all. Sending a link to your mom. I'm quite proud of you for this.*

He couldn't help but smile at his grandmother's text, even though she was going to share it with his mother. Of course, Fred might have already done that. He knew exactly what time the whole scheme was going to go down.

Eddie hadn't been being cute when he named what they were doing *Operation Tell the World I Read Romance*. His whole world was about to know that he had changed his mind about romance novels – no, no, that wasn't right. He wasn't the one who had changed his mind; it was Ava. The frustrating, happily-ever-after-loving romance writer who had hired him to edit her books and, in the process, had captured his heart.

"Wait. You're recommending Ava's romances?" Lacey asked as she stared at the sign.

"I am."

"Have you read them?"

"Each and every one," he admitted. "And I liked them all."

"He's her editor now, too," Josh added as if it was the most important secret he knew.

"You are?" Eddie thought Lacey's eyeballs might pop out of her head with as wide as her eyes were opened. "So this is the secret?"

"It is. I read and edit romance – those written by Ava. I haven't read any others yet, but I think I might read a couple just so I can truly see how good she is." He knew from what he had read that she was a good author. In fact, it had surprised him that she was as good as she was at first because he had thought that romance writers were just writers who didn't have what it took to write other things. Some of the movies his mom and sister watched seemed to support that theory.

He propped the first book from each of Ava's series on book stands on top of the case. "I'm also rather fond of this author as a person." His ears were burning. But if Ava could tell everyone that she wrote romance, he would tell everyone he read romance – her romance books – and that she was special to him.

Looking towards the computer room, he saw Ava heading his direction.

"That's all the books," Josh said. "They're all in order and everything."

Eddie stepped back to look at the full display. "Looks good, doesn't it?" He turned toward Lacey and looked from her to the shelving cart.

She shook her head. "Oh, no. I'm not leaving now. I need to see what Ava thinks. Too bad Trish isn't here." She snapped a picture of the display and then took a closeup of the display sign.

"Can you send those to Fred, too?"

Lacey turned a questioning look towards him. "Sure, if you want me to, but you know he'll share it with everyone."

"That's the plan," Josh said.

"Plan?" Lacey repeated.

Josh nodded as Ava joined them.

"This…" She shook her head and just held up her phone as if she couldn't form words. "So sweet."

"And true. Every word of it." He took her by the shoulders and turned her toward the display they had just finished. "If you can share yourself with the world, so can I. So, I'm outing myself," he whispered by her ear.

She gasped and then read the sign out loud. "*Books that will make you believe in happily ever after, penned by local author, Ava Johnston, and heartily recommended by Edmund Bennett, a member of Hatfield Falls' library team.* Oh, Eddie." She brushed at her tears. "Do you mean it? Do you really believe in happily ever afters?"

"As you define them? Yes. I still think that they aren't real by my definition, but then, my definition might not be right."

She threw her arms around his neck and hugged him tightly. "Yes, yes, yes, I would gladly change the name of my blog to *An Author Writing Her Own Happily Ever After* if you're serious about forgiving me for acting without thinking."

"What is she talking about?" he heard Lacey whisper.

"This," Ava handed Lacey her phone.

"You might want to wait to give me your answer on that," Eddie said. "There's one more piece to this happily ever after that I'm trying to edit for you."

That's how he had started his reply to her blog post: "*As your editor and intimately acquainted with both you and Library Guy (since I'm him), I find this ending to your romance story unsatisfying. Below are my thoughts and suggestions on how I think it could be resolved in a way that I would find quite to my liking...*"

He had then shared his thoughts on the heroine of her story – her – and how much the hero of her story – him – did not want their story to end with a parting of ways.

"And that would be?"

Eddie heard the door to the library open.

"He's here," Josh whispered.

He saw Ava's gaze move away from him and to the door.

"Why is Sam here?" Ava demanded.

"I know who his library source is, and he agreed to come share it with you."

"How do you know?"

"I went to see him on Tuesday, right before I came to the library and Josh helped me plan this." He waved a hand at the display before taking her hand and leading her towards the story time room.

"I thought we could talk in private in here." He opened the door and allowed both Sam and Ava to enter ahead of him. "It won't take too long, but I thought it would be best for you to hear this from Sam and not me."

"Hi," Sam said. "Seems I made things worse with you and not better." He gave her a sheepish grin.

Eddie had been surprised to discover that behind the bravado that Sam had worn last week at the library, there was a guy who actually cared about things outside of himself. It hadn't happened automatically, but after hearing how Ava had responded to his article, the shutters had opened and the somewhat softer side of Sam had revealed, and apparently, he was a quick study and going to let the vulnerability show through again today. Unless, of course, this was all just a part of how a player played. It wasn't as if Eddie was going to suddenly trust the guy around females or share his secrets with him.

"I didn't realize that your identity as a writer was a secret until your boyfriend came to see me. Honestly, I wasn't trying to make some grand reveal or hurt you. I had hoped that my words in that article would help atone for some of the pain I caused in the past. I didn't know how deeply I had injured you until I saw you that day in the computer room, and you were still bristling all these years later. I am honestly sorry for treating you like I did. I was a stupid kid, and, as it turns out, I'm also a stupid adult who is working on being less stupid."

"How did you know who I was?" Her arms were crossed in a defensive pose, but she didn't look angry so much as unsure of herself.

Eddie hated that what had happened all those years ago still did this to her.

"Your laptop was open to your blog, and I saw a book in the bag next to the leg of your chair. It was enough for me to start a search." He shrugged. "I've always been good at puzzles – even tricky ones. You had yourself fairly well hidden."

She sank backwards. "I was your source?"

He nodded.

She shook her head. "And I blamed you, when it was me." She had turned to Eddie. "I've been such an idiot!" Her sigh sounded like a great weight falling from her shoulders. "Thank you, Sam. Gran – Eddie's grandmother – pointed out how your article was flattering. I'm glad you enjoyed the books you read."

"About that. Book two – the creep – it's me, isn't it?" he asked.

Ava shrugged and smiled. "Oh, no. To avoid being dubbed humiliating names, I no longer share my inspirational sources for characters. Not even in my notes."

He chuckled. "Ava the Forlorn," he said as he shook his head. "But you're not forlorn. You've got a pretty great guy. Being forlorn is my role now. And from your answer, I'm just going to assume that I inspired the creep – whom," he added as he reached for the doorknob, "I believe you call Sir Jerk-a-lot?"

Her eyes grew wide, and she turned to Eddie.

"He didn't tell me anything. I read your blog," Sam said. "All of it. You're a very good writer, Ava." And with that, he left the room.

"So what do you think?" Eddie asked. "Are you still considering the blog name change?"

She nodded as she turned to face him. "I'll consider it if you'll be my happy for now."

Eddie shook his head. "Nope. I'm not ready to get down on one knee or anything – we've only had one date – but I'm still not planning to settle for being anything other than your happily ever after, because I can't imagine my future as happy without you."

She wrapped her arms around his neck, and he circled her waist with his. "I think I like the sounds of that. You're a very good editor."

He smiled. "I know."

She chuckled. "Then, you likely know how this scene is supposed to end?"

He nodded.

Her brow furrowed. "So are you going to kiss me?"

"I'm not the romance writer. I'm just the editor. You're going to have to give me something to work with here."

She laughed and shook her head before saying, "And they lived happily ever after," as her lips came to rest on his.

A spark of something fiery and thrilling shot through him at the touch and as beautifully as words flowed from her pen and as easily as he found the little tweaks that needed to happen to enhance their beauty, their kiss left the realm of the light and teasing and settled into something far more intimate as they stepped into what he knew would be their very own – but never perfectly without difficulties – happily ever after.

Chapter 20

A Step Towards New Beginnings

The hero of Hatfield Falls (Don't Tell) Book 4 is Frederick. He's been best friends with Esther since they were ten. Below is a scene that will give you a peek into their relationship and how for one of them, that friendship might be morphing into something more.

Esther hummed through the melody of the song on the sheet in front of her while the rest of the worship team picked out their parts on their own. Fred strummed softly on his guitar as he listened to her hum. This was what he hoped heaven sounded like – a cacophony of people preparing to praise their Lord and then, a fantastic set of songs once they began their performance.

Not that it was a performance, he corrected himself. How many times had he heard his dad admonish him that he was a worship leader and not a worship performer?

More than once, he thought with a chuckle. And yet, it still felt like a performance more often than not.

"Ready to perform for Jesus?" he asked Esther as she got to the end of her sheet music.

"I'm always ready to perform, but don't you think it sounds a bit..." Her nose wrinkled as her face took on her thinking expression – the same one that had made him tease her in grade four and started what was now a lifelong friendship.

He wrinkled his own nose.

"Stop that!" She smacked him with her music. "We're nearly a quarter of a century old. You think you'd have stopped teasing me about how I think by now."

He laughed. "Never. It's cute."

"Teasing is not cute, Frederick Bennett."

She had slipped into her teacher voice.

"Yes, Miss Adams. Sorry, Miss Adams." But the way she did that thing with her nose was cute.

She laughed and swatted him with her music once more. "As I was saying, I think it sounds a bit commercial to call what we're doing a performance – even if you say it is for Jesus. It's not like He's paying us to do it."

Well, that was true. "But it does feel like getting ready for a concert at school or something, and those, even without being paid, were performances."

"Oh, you got paid." She accepted a handheld mic with fresh batteries from the sound guy. "It was called a grade."

"Yes, Miss Adams." He plugged his guitar into the amp. "So what would you call what we're doing then?"

"Practice." She fluttered her lashes at him. "I'm surprised you didn't know that since you texted me about bringing your sweater back to you at practice tonight."

His light grey, zip-up hoodie, which he had given her to wear when her soda had spilled and soaked her shirt last Sunday during the Grey Cup watching party, was folded neatly and sitting on one of the chairs in the front row – precisely in the middle of the chair. It was how Esther did things – to perfection. Nothing was thrown together or slapped into place. She was meticulous. It was a wonder the two of them were such good friends, because he was not so detail oriented as she was – except when it came to cars. There, he was as picky as picky could be. Being creative and taking risks was not something one did when working on an engine or bolting on a tire. In the garage, there was only one way to do something – the right way.

The doors to the auditorium opened, and Esther waved to the newcomer.

"Ava's here?"

"Yep. I invited her to see how things are done here. She worked on the soundboard at her last church, so I suggested that she should consider doing that here." She turned to Fred with a mischievous grin. "I suggested it before she and Eddie got together this week because I thought it might give them a chance to serve together and maybe become more than friends."

"That was a good idea. Wish I had thought of it."

"Well, we can't all be me," she said with a laugh.

"We're ready back here." The sound guy stood in the sound booth and made a circling motion with his finger to tell them it was time to get things together and this practice over with.

"Are we still going to the diner for fries after? Or did you plan something with Ava?"

"I hoped she would come with us. Maybe you can have Eddie meet us there? He should be done with work by then."

Fred sighed. "I suppose." He wasn't sure he wanted to share their tradition with his brother and his brother's girlfriend – no matter how much he liked his brother or how great Ava was. Fries at the diner after practices were his and Esther's thing. Still, he texted Eddie since he didn't want to disappoint Esther.

"I think how you helped him with his surprise for Ava was really sweet."

"Thanks." But nope, that wasn't going to make him feel any better about sharing his and Esther's tradition with Eddie.

"I can't believe she writes the books I love so much."

"Any time now," the sound guy called from the back.

Fred began playing the intro to "This is Amazing Grace" while Esther moved closer to the keyboard, which was where she always stood when she sang.

Four songs later, with two of them requiring two passes to get things nailed down, Fred found himself packing up his guitar.

"Did you hear back from Eddie?"

"Yep. He'll meet us there in about fifteen minutes, and he gave me his order just in case. However, that's only if Ava is coming."

"Oh, she'll come. I'm sure she will."

"I don't know. It's getting late, and she has to drive home."

"Wilson's Crossing isn't that far from the diner." Esther headed towards the back of the auditorium, and before he had finished zipping up his guitar case, she was giving him an exuberant thumbs up.

Great. Just awesome. He trudged through the sanctuary and into the foyer. Esther and Ava were already on their way out the front door.

"You guys sounded great tonight," his dad said from where he sat outside the door to the church office.

"Thanks."

"Ava seemed to enjoy herself." His dad tipped his head and studied Fred. "It's good to see her finding a place to fit in here."

He nodded. "It is." What did his dad want? He never used that tipped head scrutiny look unless he was fishing for information.

"And yet, you don't look very happy about that."

Fred shook his head. "Just caught up in my thoughts. I'm happy she enjoyed herself. I really am."

"Mom wanted to come with me tonight."

Ah, he was fishing on Mom's behalf. That made sense.

"She hasn't seen you since Eddie and Ava decided to make their relationship known to one and all in a very public way."

Fred's brow furrowed. "Why does she need to see me? I didn't do anything that Eddie didn't ask me to do." Of course, he had suggested a couple of things that were on that list, but still he had only done them because Eddie had been okay with it.

"You and your brother are no longer just a duo. A third person has been added to the mix – a person who might always come between you and Eddie. As she should – in a proper sort of fashion, but I think you know what I mean."

"I'm okay with it, Dad. I'm one hundred percent happy for him." He had even encouraged Eddie to pursue the relationship when his brother was doing his normal question things to death about liking Ava. He knew that things would change between them. Things already were, and while he didn't always like it, he was happy for his brother. "In fact, he and Ava are going to join us at the diner for fries." Not that he was okay with that, but it seemed like a good example to share to prove that he was happy for Eddie.

His dad stood. "Well, don't let me keep you from your date."

"It's not a date, Dad. It's a tradition."

His father chuckled. "Your mother would be happier if I could tell her it was a date."

Fred laughed. "You can tell her that I'm not jealous of Eddie and Ava, and that I'm still free and single and that, unlike Will, I'll let her know when that changes."

Again, his father chuckled. "You would think she'd be content to have three of her boys either married or on their way to it, but she's not." He held the door open for Fred. "Have fun at the diner. I'll pass your message on to your mother."

Fred's car was just starting to get toasty warm when he pulled into the parking lot at the Falls Diner and turned it off. Eddie pulled in behind him.

"Hey, you're early," Fred said to him as he got out of his car.

"I had a good incentive to hurry." Eddie shrugged and smiled as if he wasn't sure if he should be so sappy. Fred didn't mind. Henry, Brandon, or Will might tease Eddie for such a comment, but he wouldn't. He knew his twin didn't admit things like that easily – or, at least, he never would have before he met Ava.

"Who's that talking to Esther?"

Fred looked through the plate glass window to the booth he and Esther always sat in after a worship team practice. There, leaning against the side of the bench where Esther was sitting, was some good-looking blonde guy. "I have no idea, but I guess we'll find out."

He held the door for his brother and then followed behind Eddie while observing Mr. Chatty at the booth. The guy certainly seemed familiar with Esther and happy to be so.

"Hello," Eddie said as he reached the table.

"Hi," the stranger replied. "Wow! You guys definitely are twins. Miss Adams and her friend were just telling me that they were waiting for you." He stuck out his hand to Eddie. "Steve White. I have a child at Miss Adams's school."

"Edmund Bennett," Eddie said as he shook Steve's hand.

"Fred Bennett," Fred said when it was his turn.

"I won't keep you from your fries. Madison won't be happy if I'm not home to read her a bedtime story – although she might forgive me if I tell her that I was talking to her favourite teacher."

Esther laughed lightly. "Tell, Maddie *hello* for me."

"Will do. It was a pleasure to meet you all."

"Does this happen a lot? Parents just come up and talk to you?" Ava asked once Steve was out of earshot.

"More often than I would like," Esther replied. "I taught his daughter last year. They had just moved here after a messy divorce, and Madison struggled a bit to settle into her new surroundings, but her dad's great so it wasn't too long before she was just one of the crowd. Mom's not great – or so I've heard from Steve and his daughter. It's not that they have told me straight out, but I've learned a few things in snatches of conversation. I kind of know what to listen for." She lifted one shoulder in a half shrug. Fred knew that Esther wasn't just talking from teacher training or something – she had personal experience with a parent who wasn't great.

"Have you guys had lots of conversations other than at parent-teacher things?"

Fred also wanted to know that answer to Ava's question. Because Mr. Steve White seemed a whole lot more friendly than a casual acquaintance.

"Actually, we have. He's a nice guy." She leaned forward and whispered. "He hasn't asked me out yet, but now that his daughter isn't in my class..." She let the thought trail off.

"Can you date a parent?" Fred asked in surprise. Surely, that must go against some sort of policy somewhere.

"According to my principal, if they don't have a student in my class, or if the relationship began before the child became my student, I can."

"And you'd go out with him if he asked you?" This night was just spiraling into all sort of unwelcome things – first he had to agree to share this time with Eddie and Ava.

Then, his father had questioned him for his mother, and now, Esther was thinking about dating some guy who was a father?

"I don't know. Maybe. I mean, I'd like to get married some day, so dating someone needs to happen sometime."

"Well, yeah, but how old is he, and are you sure that it wasn't his fault that his wife took off?" He grimaced as the words came out of his mouth since they were hitting pretty close to the divorce history in Esther's family life. "I mean it could be. Doesn't mean that it is, but, like, what do you know about him?"

"I think that's what dating is for – to find out about someone." There was an edge to her reply. "He's not even thirty yet. He got married straight out of high school – well, a year and a half after grad, but that's pretty much straight out of school." She again leaned toward Ava and whispered. "And he's cute, right?"

"Sure is," Ava agreed.

"In a parental sort of way," Fred grumbled.

Esther elbowed him. "Be nice. I kind of like him."

"Seriously?"

"Yes. Now, can you please wave Pam over so we can order our fries? I told her you'd signal when we were ready so that she didn't have to keep coming around and asking."

Fred blew out a breath and lifted his arm to wave at Pam. This was not how this night was supposed to go. He and Esther were supposed to have slipped into this booth and laughed and talked about music or life or whatever while eating fries. Alone. Just the two of them. Eddie and Ava were not supposed to be across the booth from them, and that guy – Steve – Fred barely refrained from rolling his eyes as he thought the name – was not supposed to be here, nor was he supposed to be someone Esther liked.

Read Fred and Esther's story in Hatfield Falls (Don't Tell)
Book 4, *Don't Tell My Best Friend I Love Her*.
Join one of Annilee's reader communities for updates on Fred and Esther's story and everything else Hatfield Falls.

About Annilee

Annilee Nelson writes faith-filled sweet romances from a cozy corner in the living room of her just-outside-of-Halifax-Nova-Scotia home. She is a life-long lover of stories with her favorite sorts being those that include families, groups of friends, and, of course, romance. Like Mrs. Bennett in the Hatfield Falls series, Annilee loves Jane Austen, though not enough to name her children after Miss Austen's characters.

Find out how to connect with Annilee, learn about her books and Nova Scotia (the setting for Hatfield Falls), and get a copy of the story of the day Mr. Bennett proposed to his wife at https://bit.ly/Annilee_Subscribe